Petals and Nails

Petals and Nails

A
Novella
by
Loni Hoots

2018

Petals and Nails: A Novella
Copyright © 2018 by Loni Hoots
All rights reserved.

ISBN 978-1-7325023-1-4

Edited by Gloria J. Wimberley
Front cover design by Loni Hoots

Published by Middle Island Press
PO Box 354
West Union, WV 26456

Petals and Nails

Chapter 1

STANDING IN THE MIDDLE OF NOWHERE in the dead of winter with the snow falling was the scene that was stuck inside Ingrid's mind. However, she was sitting on the couch with a blanket draped over her lap and a hot mug of coffee in her hands. The television set shined brightly in the dark living room, paving a bright pathway directed towards Ingrid. The sounds of a Lifetime movie played, and the voices bounced off the walls, creating a unique, beautiful vibration and waking her out of the trance. Shaking her head, she raised the mug up to her lips and slowly sipped the hot coffee, letting it slide down her throat smoothly, letting it warm every inch of her. Looking at her mobile phone, she could see that it was only 1 am on a Saturday morning. Placing the phone beside her on the couch, she reached forward with her mug and placed it on the coffee table. Pulling off the blanket and throwing it to the side of her, she slowly got off the couch and started down the long, narrow, dark hallway towards the bathroom. Flipping on the bathroom light, she made her way over to the sink and turned on the faucet. Adjusting the water temperature, she pulled her long, wavy, red hair into a ponytail and scrunched up her long sleeves to prevent them from getting wet. Once the water was the right temperature, she splashed her face with water, then grabbed a bar of cherry-scented soap and began lathering her face. Placing the bar back onto the side of the sink, she reached back under the faucet and grabbed more water to splash onto her face again. With her eyes still closed, her hands reached for the knobs and turned them off, and then she reached for a towel and dried the water from her face. Her eyes made their way to the mirror. Undoing the pony tail, her wavy red hair fell over her shoulders as her eyes fixed upon her reflection. Studying herself, she could see the bright blue eyes she inherited from her mom, and her hair too. She saw the countless freckles on her face. One time she tried to count every freckle but was unable to. She could see the full oval face she inherited from her dad, and the nose from him as well. Being on the short side, her physique looked curvier yet proportional. Overall, she was a very pretty woman, twenty-eight years old.

Walking out of the bathroom, Ingrid turned off the light and was at once greeted by the dark hallway. She slowly made her way back to the living room to finish the movie. She plopped down on-to the couch, draped the blanket back over her lap and grabbed her mug. The commercials stopped playing and the movie began again. Once again, her mind went into a trance-like state. This time, she saw herself on the shore of Iceland and was looking out at the dark, icy, blue ocean water. In her mind, she wanted to take a dip, but in this state, her body and mind wouldn't let her do it. Instead, she just kept staring out into the ocean, watching the waters wade back and forth.

In an instant, the brightness of the screen had caught Ingrid off guard and awakened her out of the trance, and she was brought back again into reality. As she sat there watching the actors say the lines and engage in high-speed chases, she began to think about her life in Iceland.

She was born in Keflavik, to Isobel and Arthur Anderssen. But when she was seven years old, they moved to Shannon, Ireland, where her younger brother Eli was born. Four years later, they relocated back to Keflavik. Ingrid stayed until it was time for her to pursue college. She ended up going to Holar University College majoring in equine studies. Always fascinated with horses, Ingrid decided she wanted to make a career of working with them.

In an instant, the screen changed and the credits began to roll up the television set. Glancing down at her mobile, she noticed that it was nearing two in the morning. Turning off the television, she threw the blanket off, grabbed the mug and her phone and ventured down the dark hallway once again. Finally reaching the kitchen, she flipped the light on and walked to the sink to pour out the coffee and rinse the mug. Placing the mug inside the sink, Ingrid began to think back to when she was graduating from the university.

It was the last semester, and things in her personal life weren't going too well. Her grades were perfect and she was at the top of her class and was thrilled about that, but she had just ended a four-year relationship because of infidelity. She couldn't cope with it, so she ended the relationship and never did anything outside of her classes. She didn't know exactly what she was going to do after graduation until she was offered a job over in Hellnar at a ranch.

The offer was amazing! She could work with an incredible family and with some of the most beautiful horses in the west of Iceland. She found a small home where she would be able to rent for a good price. Once she graduated, she got out of Holar and headed to Hellnar to start a new life. And here she was, four years later, settled into a home that she bought with the money she saved, and was still working at the ranch that she dearly loved.

Walking out of the kitchen, she turned off the light and made her way to the bedroom. As she stood in the doorway, her eyes fixed on the queen-sized bed. Every night and morning, it was just her under the blankets in the fetal position to keep herself warm. She was still single—the only one single in her group of friends. Ingrid always had a hard time going to bed when she didn't have anyone that she loved to come home to, or go to bed with, or wake up next to. She always woke up with her heart aching and soul hurting, knowing that she would never find love. She made her way to the bed and crawled under the covers. Grabbing the charger, she plugged the phone in and placed it on the nightstand. Placing her head onto the pillow, it didn't take long for her to fall fast asleep.

Chapter 2

INGRID AWAKENED to morning light coming into the room. Adjusting her eyes to the light, she grabbed the phone from the nightstand to look at the time. The time was displayed in a bright red color: 10 o'clock. It was alright since she didn't work at the ranch on Saturdays or Sundays. During those days, the family wanted the children to learn how to take care of the horses (that way, they knew what to do if no one was around). Ingrid had no complaints; she thoroughly enjoyed having the weekend off. It gave her time to do whatever she wanted. Most of the time she ended up reading in her own little library, and other times she would visit her family.

Today, the only thing on her mind was going for a drive, any-where, just to get away and see what was out there in the wild parts of Iceland. After crawling out of bed, Ingrid made her way to the bathroom. Stripping off her pajamas, she turned the shower on, filling the bathroom air with a thick, lingering fog, and stepped inside the shower. Letting the hot water run down her hair and body, Ingrid just stood there for a few minutes before shampooing and conditioning her hair. Once that was done, she lathered and rinsed her body. Turning off the water and opening the curtain, a wave of cold air hit her skin, sending shivers down her body.

Quickly grabbing a towel, she wrapped herself in it and stood in front of the sink and mirror. Wiping off the fog that covered the mirror, she reached for the brush and began brushing her hair, hitting a snag every so often. Once done, she left the bathroom with the light still on and walked back to the bedroom to put on warm clothes. Slipping into her underwear and bra, she considered the options in the closet and pulled out a pair of jeans, a long-sleeved shirt and a sweater. After pulling on the clothes, she went to the dresser for a pair of socks and sat down on her bed to put them on, followed by the boots that were placed beside the bed. Walking back to the bathroom, she brushed her teeth and rinsed her mouth. Turning off the light, she walked down the hallway towards the kitchen to pour coffee into her traveler's mug. Sipping slowly on the fresh hot coffee, she grabbed her purse, her keys, and jaunted out the front door, locking it behind her. Walking to her truck, she unlocked it and got in to warm up.

Turning the ignition on, she cranked the heater on and buckled up, throwing her purse in the passenger's seat. She slowly backed out of the driveway and turned down the road to head out of town. The snow filled fields and lightly-dusted roads, creating whole new scenery: A wonderland that seemed to stretch for miles. Ingrid enjoyed this due to the snow having a calming effect on her ever since she was a child. Driving down the road, there was nothing but silence. Silence filled the morning air, and silence filled the interior of the truck. The only thing that could be heard was Ingrid's breathing and the sound of the heater warming the truck.

The long road seemed to drag on, but she wasn't complaining. In fact, she found this quite soothing. She enjoyed the long, isolated roads that seemed to go anywhere. It meant new adventures, new discoveries, and new meanings to life would be found while driving on these roads. Everyone explores this side of the isolated road. This is where they tend to figure out who they are. Ingrid knew this all too well, since she had done this several times in high school and college. She ended up finding herself repeatedly. Here she was once again, except this time she was trying to force it, trying to force her future to come to her. She was trying to force what she wanted to see and feel, but it was as if the universe was saying it wasn't time yet. Ingrid kept trying to force it, but each time she kept getting irritated because it wasn't coming up. While she kept getting more irritated and angry, she kept thinking that maybe she should try to clear her mind thoroughly. But she was unable to. The driving was keeping her mind preoccupied with the road and the snow. She didn't want to crash and flip the truck over while she tried to zone out. Continuing down the long road, the snow seemed to get deeper on each side, creating a half-tunnel effect with the road in the middle. It was a gray-covered sky, disguising the sun from potential snow melting and creating a slushy effect on the road. But since it was January, the snow would not melt even if the sun appeared.

Just as Ingrid reached for the radio dial, something inside her told her to make a left at the next intersection. At first, she shook it off and turned the radio channel to another one and turned it up. The sounds of smooth jazz music filled the cabin of the truck, filling her heart with joy. Overwhelmingly, that feeling came back to her. *Turn left.* Finally caving in, she decided to turn left at the intersection. With the intersection coming into view, she flipped on the turning signal and put her foot on the brake to prepare to turn without sliding all over the road.

After making the turn, her mind went back to the radio that filled her ears with sweet sounds of guitar notes playing. As the guitar continued to play on the radio, that feeling kicked in again. This time, it came at her like a ton of bricks. *Turn left.* Yet again, the feeling said to turn left. Where was this feeling taking her? She was becoming intrigued yet worried. As she made the turn, the feeling came back. This time it was the final direction. *Stay straight.* Without questioning this feeling, she just kept driving.

Then, a sign came into view. The sign was for the parking lot for the ocean. Slowly pulling into the parking lot that was filled with compacted snow, Ingrid looked around to see where she could park without anyone ramming into her truck, or letting herself get stuck in the parking lot. Pulling into a space, she left the truck running for a moment before turning it off. She turned the key in the ignition, and the truck turned off and the heater went along with it. Unbuckling herself, she scanned the area, trying to see if there was anyone or anything near, but there was no one around. It was just herself in this isolated parking lot, over-looking the icy cold ocean.

Opening the door, a blast of cold air kissed her skin, waking her from the warmth that once enveloped her. Jumping onto the snow-packed ground, she shut the door behind her, leaving the purse and phone inside and only bringing her keys with her. Slowly, she started to walk away from the parking lot and toward the icy blue ocean.

Trudging through the snow, she didn't pay it much attention, nor the cold, brisk air. Her attention was focused on the ocean. As she got closer, she started to see the different hues of gray and blue of the ocean water. Then suddenly, she stopped. She just stood there, breathing in the fresh air, listening to the wind whispering a sweet melody in her ear, and she watched the waves wade back and forth, putting her into a trance.

It appeared that she was meditating while standing. It appeared that she was no longer near the ocean, but in a completely different place. She wasn't afraid. No. She was extremely comfortable with what was going on. She felt as though a weight had been lifted and it made her happy. It had been a while since she had been happy. The last time was two years ago, when she went on a blind date with an old friend. But when that date went south, she went numb. All her emotions just disappeared and her heart closed. She still had love for her family and helping others, but she had no love for herself. It seemed that she lost herself in this crazy world. But who doesn't lose themselves from time to time?

Taking a deep breath, Ingrid scanned the waters before walking back to the truck. Opening the door, she felt her stomach grumble, telling her that she needed food soon. Closing the door, Ingrid thought about a specific restaurant back in Hellnar: Primus Kaffi, the unique café where her favorite meals were served.

Turning the key in the ignition, Ingrid was once again greeted by the warmth of the heater. Buckling up, she made sure that the truck was ready to get back on to the snow-filled road. Putting the truck into drive, Ingrid slowly made her way out of the parking lot, and then turned back onto the road. Following the road, she made the correct turns that led her to the ocean, but in reverse, back to town. After reaching Hellnar, after an hour of driving, she continued to take the road that led to the café.

Finally reaching the café, she pulled into the parking lot, her mouth salivating with hunger. Finding a spot, she pulled in and parked the truck and turned the ignition off. Grabbing her purse and phone, along with the keys, Ingrid opened the door and jumped down. Closing the door and locking the truck, she made her way to the café.

Chapter 3

OPENING THE CAFÉ'S DOOR, the sound of a bell rang, causing the woman behind the counter to acknowledge her. The woman looked at Ingrid with a warm smile, greeting her with a sense of comfort. Ever since Ingrid moved here, she always made it a weekly mission to stop by the café. Walking up the counter, Ingrid glanced up at the menu and selected what she wanted.

"Hello, Ingrid."

"Hello, Maria."

"What do you want to get today?"

"The soup of the day sounds good. Also, I'll have water."

"Good choice. I'll bring it out to you when it's ready. Go ahead and have a seat."

Walking away from the counter, Ingrid's eyes locked on an empty table in the corner. Strolling over to the table, she could see people in different spots: A guy with glasses reading a book while eating a sandwich and sucking down an iced tea, and an elderly couple enjoying a lunch date; giggling, having a wonderful time. A smile crept across her face as she walked to the table. *All these people must be in love. These people must have fascinating lives,* she thought to herself. *What do they do? Do they lead adventurous lives?* She continued to think to herself.

Sitting down at the table, she tried to answer these questions in her mind, but she was unable to. It appeared that her mind wanted to take her to a different place: Once again, back to that isolated place, somewhere in the middle of nowhere, that place where all is quiet. Where there is nothing for miles. Where time, for just a moment, stops…and you can breathe without anything weighing you down. Where all regrets, pains, sorrows, anger are gone from the soul and body, leaving a person with nothing but happiness.

Again, she was shocked out of her trance. A bowl of soup, a plate of bread, and a glass of water were placed in front of her.

"Here you go, dear!" Maria said to her.

"Thank you."

Maria walked away, leaving Ingrid staring into the bowl of soup in front of her. Stirring the soup with a spoon, she continued to stare at it with a lot of focus. Finally lifting the spoon to her mouth, she let the ingredients fill her mouth and savored each bite. As she continued to eat, the young man in the glasses who was reading looked up from the book and just stared for a minute. He studied Ingrid, trying to figure her out. After a moment, he took his eyes off her and went back to his book.

For a second, as she was eating, Ingrid thought someone had been watching her. But then that feeling went away. As she continued to eat the soup and bread, she couldn't think of anything else. The warmth of the soup penetrated her thoughts. It let the steam create a unique sensation and keep her focused on the soup that was before her. Then something caught her off guard. She had that feeling once again, the feeling of someone watching her. She didn't know why and didn't know who could be watching her, but her intuition was correct.

The young man with the glasses stared up at her again. This time he studied her even longer, studying her face, her body language, her unique aura. Something about her seemed familiar, yet he could not put a finger on it. After a few more minutes, he looked down at his book, took a sip out of his mug and placed a bookmark inside his book. Standing up, he grabbed his book, glanced at Ingrid once more, and then proceeded to walk toward the front door. Leaving the café, he walked toward his truck in the parking lot.

Back inside the café, Ingrid continued eating her soup. She did not let on that she had continuously had her own eyes on the young man. She could see out of the corner of her eye that he was staring at her, but she did not want to create a scene. She did not want to give the impression that she was a little scared, so she focused on her soup while keeping an eye on him. Once he left, Ingrid could finally relax and finish her meal.

As she took the last sip out of her glass, she pushed the empty bowl away from her. Setting the glass down, she stood up, grabbed her purse and walked toward the counter to pay for the meal. Once she reached the counter, the front door rang open and a sound of footsteps came up behind Ingrid.

"I'll be with you in a moment, dear." Maria said to the person behind Ingrid.

"Thank you," a young man's voice responded.

"Okay, the total will be 998 krona."

Ingrid reached inside her purse to pull out the money.

"Out of 1,010?" the lady spoke. "Here you go, here is your change."

"Thank you. Have a great day," Ingrid said as she began to turn around.

"You too, stay safe."

Ingrid turned around to be greeted by the young man from earlier.

"Oh, hello there," the young man spoke.

"Hello, how are you?" Ingrid asked as she studied his face.

"I'm doing well, thank you. Just forgot something."

"Ah, okay. I must go, but have a good day."

As Ingrid walked toward the front door, she had that feeling again. Opening the door, she turned her head toward the counter to see the young man looking back at her. Their eyes locked, and both smiled. Ingrid walked out the door, leaving him staring at the door, and then his attention was shifted.

"Hello, dear. What did you need?" Maria asked.

"I forgot my notebook. Do you have it?" he asked.

"Yes, I was going to call you to give it to you."

"I realized that I had forgotten it half a mile down the road," he chuckled.

"It happens to all of us, dear."

"All the time for me," he said, laughing.

He thanked her, held the notebook in one hand, and waved as he walked through the door. The bell rang as the door opened wide, letting the cool Icelandic air into the café.

He trudged through the snow, back to his truck, and climbed in, closed the door and started up the truck. Heading out of the parking lot, he headed toward the outside of the town, back to his home. Throughout the drive down the snow-covered road, the sound of silence filled the cabin of his truck since his stereo was broken. He kept telling himself that he would fix it soon, but it always seemed to be later than sooner.

Driving down the road, he noticed a vehicle up ahead that seemed to be stuck in the snow, and the driver was trying to get out of the deep snow bank. Pulling up next to the truck, he left his vehicle running and got out to check on the driver.

Chapter 4

THE TRUCK'S DOOR OPENED and Ingrid jumped down to be greeted by the man from the café. Her face was already flushed and slightly pink from the air, but seeing him being the one to come to her rescue made her face flush even more.

"What happened here?" he asked, looking at her and the truck.

"I was trying to shift gears and I didn't slow down enough to do that, and I lost control and went straight into the bank."

"Oh, wow. Well, I have supplies in my truck and I'll help you get out."

"Thank you."

"Very welcome. I'm Mathew."

"I'm Ingrid. Nice to meet you, Mathew."

"Go ahead and get into your truck and put it into neutral."

Ingrid got into her truck and watched Mathew go to his truck, open the door and pull out the rope. He tied one end to the back of his truck and the other end to the front of her truck. He got back into his truck and put it into drive. Slowly putting his foot on the gas pedal, he started forward. Her truck jerked for just a moment before giving into the force of his truck. Finally, her truck was out of the bank and they both stopped on the side of the road. Mathew got out of his truck, as did Ingrid, and they met where the rope was.

"I'll follow you to your house, just to make sure you won't have another incident," he said, unhooking the rope from both trucks.

"Thank you once again, Mathew."

"So, go ahead and pull out in front of me and I'll follow you."

Ingrid walked back to her vehicle, got in and slowly made her way around his truck. By this time, Mathew had put the rope inside his truck and was already situated. He watched her truck go down the road, and he followed behind at the same pace.

After two miles, Mathew saw Ingrid's left blinker blinking, signaling to him that she had arrived at her destination. He turned his blinker on and followed her down the snow-covered driveway that led to her house. Once she stopped, so did he. Ingrid gathered her things, jumped down from her truck and noticed that his truck was still running. She closed her truck door and Mathew opened his and got down.

"Thank you once again," she said.

"Very welcome. If you ever need anything, I'm always at the café. But just in case, here is my number," he said, handing her a business card. *Mathew Refs, Veterinarian,* it read on one side, and the other side listed his mobile number, work number and email.

"Thank you, Mathew. I will call you if I need anything."

"Very welcome, Ingrid. I'd better be off now; hope to see you real soon."

Ingrid stood there as she watched him get back into his truck and head down her driveway. Once he got out of her driveway, she made her way up to the front door of the house. Unlocking the door, she was welcomed by the warmth of the heater that encased each room in a hot sauna experience. Setting everything down, she looked down the hallway.

"Hmm, I think I'll make tea and go write for a while."

She walked into the kitchen, put the tea kettle on the stove and turned it on. She grabbed a mug from the cabinet, grabbed a tea bag from her favorite canister, Lady Grey. Placing the tea bag into the mug, she looked out to the backyard. The sight of the snow piled high was her favorite scene to look at every day. And she wouldn't have it any other way.

The sound of the tea kettle whistling made her head turn from the window. Turning the stove off, she grabbed the tea kettle and poured the boiling water into the mug. While steeping the tea bag, Ingrid thought she heard something but thought it might've been the snow falling off the roof. Taking the tea bag out, she threw it into the trashcan, walked out of the kitchen and made her way down the hallway to her library. Opening the library door, she felt for the light switch with her free hand. She was greeted by the warm room filled to the ceiling with books that she had been collecting over the years. The books ranged from collector's editions to romance novels to thrillers. Most of them were given to her throughout the years for birthdays and Christmases, and the others were ones she had bought at second-hand bookstores and through her travels over the years.

Setting her mug on the side table, her eyes roamed around and locked onto the desk that was situated under the window. There she spotted the journal she needed; it was set next to her writing pens and drawing pencils. Grabbing the journal and a pen, she sat next to her mug in the soft, cushioned chair and got comfortable. Taking a sip of the tea, she looked at the journal that lay in her lap. It had been some time now since she last wrote in her journal. The last entry was dated from months ago, back in August, back when she had her nervous breakdown and had to see a therapist, and almost attempted something that she had attempted a few times before in her teenage years...suicide. It was a touchy subject that she had always tried to steer clear from. Even when she went to see the therapist, it took her nearly twenty minutes to explain what occurred. After the session, her therapist suggested that she start writing, writing about everything: What she was feeling, her day, who she met, anything and everything. Ingrid had never thought of doing that. She thought it seemed to be a bit childish, but her therapist assured her that many adults do in fact write in journals. That night, after the session, Ingrid gave it a shot. At first it seemed stupid to her, but then it became therapeutic, and then she stopped. Something inside her made her stop writing, and she didn't care.

Now here she was, months later, into a new year. Picking up the pen, opening to a blank page, she began to write:

The things we have done in the past tend to come back and haunt us. All the fear, all the nightmares start crawling back in while we are asleep in our warm beds at night. And for the most part, there is nothing we can do. Nothing can stop it. We can try to subdue it, try to make it go to sleep for a little while, and it will; but then it will emerge once again, attack us and take us down. It will make us feel as though we are powerless. Even though we might feel powerless, there is a glimmer of hope, that little spot of light on the inside that tells us that we are power-ful, that we are strong, that we are brave. Ultimately, we have a choice. Either we can listen to that light inside us, or we can continue to feel this way, continue to not fight this battle and let the disorder take a hold on us. Take over everything. Take control of our lives. Take control of our work. And take control of our love life. Dealing with this is hard, although I've dealt with it for years and it doesn't get easier. It just gets harder. There are days when I don't want to go to work and I just want to stare at the ceiling all day until I fall asleep again. Then there are days that I am just extremely happy and feel like everything in the world is working with me and not against me. I can't be the only one who feels like this, right? I can't be the only one who deals with this daily. Thankfully, there is a name for this. But it is horrifying to give it a name, because it feels like I am giving it power, I am giving it a life of its own. And I don't want it to have a much larger part in my life by giving it a name. But it is nice to know of the name, in case I want to learn more about it. In case I want to see what the doctors say about it. But for now, I will just say the name: Bipolar disorder. There, I've said it. I feel like I can only say the name in writing for right now. Maybe one day I will be able to say it out loud, be able to talk about it, be able to cope with it and sort out everything, finally. I must give it time. For as they say, time heals all wounds.

Setting the journal and pen down on her lap, she reached for the mug of tea that was still somewhat warm and sipped it slowly. The thoughts in her head were still boiling as if they were trying to jump out and throw themselves onto the page of her journal. But Ingrid was trying to calm down the thoughts by drinking the tea, and she began to think about what might be on the television. The thought of numbing herself by watching something random seemed fitting for the moment, especially since her thoughts were running wild.

Getting out of the chair and taking the mug with her, Ingrid walked out of the room while turning the light off and closed the door on her way out. Heading down the hallway towards the living room, Ingrid noticed headlights coming down her driveway. She turned the other way toward the front door and saw a truck had pulled up and a figure had started to walk toward the porch that was now covered with fresh, new snow. She sat the mug down on the side table where her keys were, turned on the front porch light and opened the door. She was greeted by a towering silhouette that was being framed by lightly fallen snow.

"Hey, Sis," the figure spoke.

"Eli!" Ingrid exclaimed, shocked. "What are you doing here?" She let him inside and closed the door behind them.

"I'm traveling back to college this weekend. May I stay the night?"

"Of course, you know you can always stay here."

"Thank you, Sis."

"Anytime. Were you coming from Mom and Dad's?" she asked as they walked down the hallway toward the living room.

"So, what were you about to do? And yeah, I spent the holidays with Mom and Dad."

"I was just about to watch some television. Did you want to take a shower tonight or wait until morning?"

"I was hoping to tonight."

"Okay, well, you know where the shower is, and do you need to go get a bag from your truck?"

"I left a set of sweats and shirt in your guestroom in case I ever came over this late."

"Oh, okay, I'll let you go take a shower. I'll be in the living room watching television."

"Okay, thank you," Eli said as he hugged her.

They separated with Eli walking to the bathroom and Ingrid going to the living room.

She plopped down on the couch, and then realized she left her mug on the side table by the front door. Getting back up, she headed down the hall and heard the water turn on, signaling to her that her brother was now in the shower. Continuing down the hall, she could see the mug in plain view. While she was by the front door, she turned off the porch light, double-checked the door to make sure that it was locked, and grabbed the mug. Heading into the kitchen, she walked over to the sink, dumped out the now-cold tea into the sink, placed the mug in the sink, and left the kitchen to head back to the living room. As she walked down the hall, the sound of the water turning off gave her a signal that her brother was done. She walked into the living room just as the bathroom door opened and Eli's footsteps retreated to the guest bedroom. She sat down on the couch and turned the television on to see that a movie was playing: Some B-rated classic movie. She didn't mind, but her brother might mind.

As the movie continued, the sound of footsteps made their way down the hall and Eli appeared through the archway of the frame that led into the room. Ingrid looked up at her younger brother. The light of the television showcased him. His tall frame standing at six feet, two inches was quite a bit different compared to her five feet, three inches. His fiery red hair was combed back and his smooth-shaven face seemed to light up from the television. The thousands of freckles all over his face had a somewhat similar pattern as Ingrid's freckles. Alongside the red hair, thousands of freckles and the face shape that they both had in common; their noses were eerily similar...they could be mistaken for fraternal twins. But she was seven years older and had blue eyes, while his were green. Just like Ingrid favored their mom in many aspects, Eli favored their dad.

Sitting next to Ingrid on the couch, Eli fixed his eyes on the screen ahead of them, and tried to figure out what was going on. From what he could gather about the movie, it was about some gangsters who were trying to find their target and kept running into dead ends each time. Eli wasn't into B-rated movies, but for the sake of spending time with his older sister, he watched the movie until he started to feel tired. It was about 10:30 at night. Eli went to bed and Ingrid was still watching television. She was now stretched out on the couch with a blanket draped over her and a pillow under her head. Feeling quite comfortable, her eyelids were trying to fight her and make her go to sleep—but Ingrid was trying to stay awake. Eventually her eyes won the battle and she fell asleep while the television continued to play.

The sweetness of slumber invited Ingrid and the dreamland started to play while vivid images create their own movie for her to watch and participate in. From what Ingrid could see so far in her dream, it was a place filled with snow and ice. No ocean this time; instead, a frost-covered forest had presented itself. Never in all her years of having dreams had a forest presented itself to her. Even in her dream presence, she was confused. Something from the forest made a sound, and shivers traveled down her spine. Unexpectedly, a fox came out, affixed his gaze on her, and motioned her to come over. Standing there, she didn't know what exactly to do…her body in the dream world started to walk towards the fox. The fox waited for a few steps, then took a few steps himself, then stopped, turned his head back to her and watched her every step. Before she knew it, she was deep inside the frozen forest with the fox. For some unknown reason, she felt safe, as if something about the forest and about the fox were keeping her safe. The fox stopped, looked at her, and darkness started to descend onto the scene, making the forest and the fox disappear, but before the fox and the entire scene vanished, he said one word to her: "Zen."

Chapter 5

THE SOUND OF FOOTSTEPS ultimately helped Ingrid wake up, but once the dream ended, she started to emerge from the dream state. She reached for her mobile phone, looked at the time and noticed that it was almost 4 o'clock in the morning. The sun not having yet risen, the darkness outside still enveloped the house. The only light she could see shined brightly from the television. From one corner of the room, she could hear a rustling sound; she could tell that it was inside the room and not outside the house. Sitting up on the couch, her eyes scanned the living room to find Eli situated in the chair and reading a book. The sound of her waking up and sitting up made him look from the book. Once he noticed that she was sitting up and almost fully awake, he just stared at her for a moment before he spoke.

"Sorry,Sis, did I wake you?"

"No, it wasn't you. It was the dream."

"What was it about?"

"Honestly, I have no clue. I'd rather not talk about it. Did you get plenty of sleep last night?" she asked, while yawning.

"Yeah, I did. The bed was so comfortable that once I put my head onto the pillow, I fell asleep instantly."

"That's good to hear. Would you like some tea or coffee? The tea kettle is on and I'm just waiting for the water to boil. Also, do you want to anything to eat? It will be a few hours till you get back to the University."

"What do you have?"

"Let me check and see what I can whip up for us. Are you hungry for something meaty and hearty, or do you want some cereal or porridge?" She asked.

"Porridge sounds good to me."

"Okay, let me go see if I still have some left," she said as she walked out of the room. The hall was so dark that she couldn't see anything below her or anything in front of her. This ultimately made her walk straight into a side table and hit her knee on it hard.

"Damn!"

The sound of her hitting the table and the sound of her voice traveled back to the living room where Eli was sitting and it made him jump out of the chair to see what happened. He found a light switch, flipped it on to find Ingrid rubbing her knee profusely.

"Are you okay?" he asked.

"Yeah, I just walked straight into the side table. I'll be fine."

She continued down the hall that was still lit up and made her way into the kitchen. The light in the kitchen was already turned on and Eli was right behind her getting ready to turn off the stove before it made the tea kettle whistle.

Rummaging through the cabinets, she came across a container that held enough porridge for both of them, so she proceeded to make the porridge just as Eli was pouring the boiling water into a mug. He found Ingrid's mug still in the sink and rinsed it for her. He rummaged through the cabinet and found a tea packet in the Lady Grey canister, placed it in the mug, and poured the boiling water inside, making the tea bag steep inside for a minute. While he was doing this, he looked over at his sister who was staring intently into the porridge. Ingrid took her eyes off the pot, went to grab two bowls for the each of them and began to pour the porridge into the bowls.

"Are you okay, Sis?" Eli asked with a confused look.

Setting the pot back onto the stove and turning the stove off, Ingrid replied, "Yes, I'm okay. Just a little tired—that's all."

"Okay, just making sure. I do worry about you."

"I know you do. I just need some more sleep."

"Once I've left, you should go back to sleep since it's Sunday."

"I was thinking about doing that," Ingrid said, yawning. "Are you ready for your classes to start up again?"

"Yes and no. I already know what classes I will be taking and some of them I love, but the others I'm not too thrilled about."

"What classes are those? The ones that you aren't thrilled about?"

"Primarily science classes. You know that I've always had a hard time with science courses."

"It'll be okay; you will do fine in those courses."

Eli was studying to be a teacher. It was something that he had always wanted to do. In fact, he knew he wanted to be a teacher since the third grade, when his teacher made a big impact on his life. Eli told his parents in high school that he had chosen his career path as an educator, and they were thrilled for him.

Ingrid and Eli each grabbed a bowl of porridge, a spoon, their mugs, and headed into the living room. Setting the mugs on the coffee table, both of their eyes fixed on the cartoon show in front of them while they slowly devoured the porridge. Here they were, brother and sister in their twenties doing the same thing that they did when they were kids: watch cartoons and enjoy breakfast. It had been a few years since they had done this. It was simple and seemed meaningless to others, but to them it was a way for them to just spend time together with only a sliver of time.

They finished their bowls and took everything back to the kitchen sink. Eli looked at his phone to see the time and realized that it was just a little after 5 o'clock, and realized he needed to get on the road. He walked to the front door with Ingrid following behind. Both put their shoes and jackets on, Eli grabbed his keys, then unlocked and opened the front door. Both were greeted by the cool morning air and the gentle wind swirled all around them. They walked outside, and Ingrid followed Eli to his truck. They said their goodbyes and hugged.

"Goodbye, Sis. I'll call you once I get to the University."

"Goodbye, Bud. Sounds good and I'll talk to you tonight. I'll call Mom and Dad to let them know that you arrived safely last night and left for the University this morning."

Eli jumped into his truck, turned the ignition on and his vehicle started up. He rolled down the window and said one last thank you before he rolled it back up and proceeded down her driveway towards the road.

Ingrid waited until he was out of sight and then walked back inside her house to be greeted by the warm air while she took off the jacket. Locking the door behind, her eyes fixated on the business card she had just received yesterday. Mathew's face entered her mind and she quickly tried to shut down that memory of him. She could remember everything that she had seen of him: His tall frame that was at least six feet, his slightly wavy brown hair, his blue eyes that were framed by his thick black glasses, and his smile that seemed very genuine and warm. This thought of him made her feel uncomfortable; she felt as though someone as nice as Mathew could never be interested in her. She felt as though there was something wrong with her, as though she was cursed and couldn't find anyone to love her as much as she could love them. She had a lot of love to give to others, but she didn't have any love for herself. She hadn't felt any love for herself in years, since the last person she dated. She felt as if she was the one who messed up, the one who was at fault, that all the blame had to fall on. But in fact, she wasn't the one who did anything wrong. It was the man who had numerous affairs and she had caught him twice. This, in turn, changed her in many ways.

As she walked down the hall, thoughts of her past started to fill her mind—things she didn't wish to face, things she didn't want to bring back to life. Instead, she just wanted to drown them out, drown her feelings with the television or while working at the ranch. For the most part, they helped, but sometimes the thoughts would sneak through and linger there. But when that occurred, Ingrid came up with a way to get her mind focused on something else. It didn't matter what it was; it just helped her get through her day-to-day life. Finding a spot on the couch, she turned the television off and just sat there for a moment before picking up her phone. Holding it in her hand, she started to dial the number to her parents' house and waited for them to pick up.

Ring! Ring! Ring!

The phone on the other end picked up and a gentle voice spoke. "Hello?"

"Hi, Mom, it's me."

"Ingrid! How are you, my darling?"

"I'm doing well. Just wanted to let you know that Eli came over late last night and left this morning for University."

"That's good to hear. He had left yesterday morning to head your way before going to University."

"How long did he stay with you?"

"About two weeks. It was nice to spend some time with him, since he has been busy with classes and work."

"Glad that you had a nice time with him. Did he get to spend time with Dad?"

"Yes, your dad did spend some good quality time with Eli when he was able to. Your dad has been pretty busy with work."

Ingrid's dad, Arthur, worked as a dentist and was very prominent back in her hometown. Her mom, Isobel, worked as an editor at a publishing company, but could work from home mostly and only had to go to the company's building three or four days out of the month for meetings or to work on group projects and get her assignments.

"That's good that they got to spend time together. Has Dad had a lot of patients lately?"

"Yes, he's been seeing ten-plus patients a day—mainly because there are only three doctors now at the clinic."

"What happened to the other three?"

"One retired and the others moved away. From what I gather, one moved to Canada and started his own business. And the other moved to Europe, because he had gotten a job offer."

"Well, I'm happy for all of them, but it must be hard for Dad and the other two. But at least they are staying busy."

"It is nice, but he does come home pretty late."

"Well, hopefully they bring another dentist in to lighten the load."

"It will be a while till that will happen. How are you doing, Dear?"

Ingrid didn't want to answer that question, but she didn't want to worry her mom, so she needed to answer in a somewhat honest way.

"I'm doing well, just working and staying busy on the ranch."

"That's good, Dear. Do you think you'll stay in Hellnar for a while longer? Or do you think you'll go somewhere else?"

"I haven't thought about it. I feel like I need to stay here and just let things take their course and continue with this ranch. They are a nice family and all of the horses seem to enjoy being around me."

"That is great, Dear. Have you made any friends or met any nice guys?"

Ingrid always hated when her mom asked her those questions. She understood that she was worried and was looking out for her. But she knew her mom knew that with her shy personality it was hard. But she did try, at least how she was able to.

"I've become acquainted with one of the ladies at the local café. And I've met a guy who had to pull my truck out of a bank of snow, and he was nice."

"That is lovely. Is he cute?"

"I don't know. I wasn't focused on his appearance; I was more focused on getting my truck unstuck." Ingrid said with a chuckle. Although she chuckled, she could not admit to her mom, let alone herself, that she found Matthew attractive. To do so would be to admit that she was developing feelings for Mathew, and she barely knew him.

"Oh, Honey, your dad is here. Do you want to say hi?"

"Sure, I haven't spoken to Dad in a couple of months."

In the background, Ingrid could hear her mom and dad exchange words, and then the phone was picked up. The sound of the voice was rougher, stronger, and heavier.

"Ingrid?" How are you, my darling daughter?"

"Hi, Dad, I'm doing well. How are you doing? I heard that you have been very busy."

"Ah, yes; my schedule has been very tight lately. Hopefully it will lighten up soon so I can have some free time."

"Are you able to have a day off?"

"Only on Sundays right now, but it's better than no days off."

"Very true. I hope you get another day off soon. You deserve it!"

"Very much so, I heard we might be getting a new dentist within a month."

"That's very good to hear. Hopefully they'll pick a person sooner."

"Fingers crossed. How is the ranch treating you?"

"The ranch is pretty amazing; the family is very kind and they keep me busy throughout the week."

"That is great, Dear. I am happy for you."

"Thank you, Dad."

For a moment there was silence on the phone. Ingrid didn't know what was going on. But on the other end, her dad was studying the sound of her voice, trying to see if she was hiding something from him. He knew his own daughter, even if she favored her mom in the physical sense. Arthur—besides being a prominent dentist and a well-respected member of the community—had the ability to detect something wrong in a person's voice and then try to help them if he thought they needed it.

The entire conversation with his daughter was not only focused on the conversation itself but also to see what she was hiding from him.

"Ingrid?"

"Yes, Dad?"

"What is wrong?"

"Nothing."

"You know you can talk about anything with me." His rough voice lowered and his natural British accent slipped through.

"I know, Dad."

"Please don't ever think you cannot come to me."

"I know that I can come to you. You've been there for me."

"Have you seen a therapist lately?"

This question didn't shock her. In fact, her dad had taken her to her first therapist when she was fifteen years old, after she made her first suicide attempt. Her dad never told her mom until Ingrid thought it was the right time. Her dad had walked in on her trying to hang herself and from that moment he sent her to a therapist to help her cope with things, to work through her problems and to help her find her strength in her weakest moments. Throughout her high school career, she went to a therapist weekly, while her brother was getting involved in sports. Once she went to college, she stopped because she thought that she had gotten better.

"I went to a therapist a few months ago, but I haven't been since."

"Is everything going okay, overall?"

"Things have gotten better, but I will have those moments where I just don't want to do anything but sleep."

"What have you been doing to help you when you haven't gone to the therapist?"

"I've been writing a little bit. It is therapeutic for me. And I'm able to just let everything out onto the page."

"Who recommended this to you?"

"It was the therapist I had seen months ago."

"I'm glad to hear that you've found a way to let your emotions and thoughts out in a more effective way."

"I am still trying to cope with everything though."

"That'll happen. I know."

When Ingrid was a freshman in college, she found out that her own dad battled with the same disorder that she had. And that was a shock to her. She had never seen him deal with problems in the same manner as she had been doing for years. But little did she know, her dad dealt with it daily. But he was better at hiding it.

He didn't want his children to see him so vulnerable, depressed to the point that he literally had to be dragged out of bed by his wife some mornings. This was what he didn't want them to see. But when Ingrid went off to college, her dad pulled her to the side and had a long talk about Bipolar Disorder and his experiences in college. He figured that it would bring awareness to her and educate her on what she might experience with the disorder. At first it scared Ingrid, then when classes started and she started dating in college, things were going up and down like a rollercoaster. She didn't know what she wanted to do. The thought of going to a therapist was at the bottom of the list, so she just decided to ride this emotional rollercoaster.

"Have you seen anyone, Dad?"

"Not lately, I've been too busy with work. But your mom and I have been able to talk every night when I come home. That helps not only me, but your mom vents as well."

"Glad you two have each other to do that."

Her dad listened to how she said that last sentence and picked up on the tone.

"You will find someone. Just focus on yourself, and then things will fall into place."

"It will take everything and everyday to focus on myself and heal. So, it will take a long time for everything to fall into place."

"You need to just heal. You need to find your Zen."

There it was again, that word: Zen. Ingrid paused and wondered why she kept hearing it and couldn't come up with a reason.

"What's wrong?" The sound of her father's voice snapped her from her mind-made trance. "Ingrid?"

"Sorry, I was just thinking about something."

"Do you want to talk about it?"

"I was just thinking about food and was thinking about going to the café."

Her dad listened intently and detected something, but he decided not to press her any further. He just let it slide. Even though she did not tell her dad what she was fully thinking about, she was indeed hungry and was thinking about getting food at the café.

"I will talk to you later this week, Dear."

"Okay dad, I'll talk to you later."

"Love you very much, and your mom loves you too."

"Love you both very much."

"Go enjoy your food and keep me updated throughout the week."

"I'll do that, Dad. Goodbye."

"Goodbye."

The phone clicked and her dad was no longer on the phone and she was once again sitting in silence. From where she was sitting on the couch, she could see out the window and see that the snow had stopped falling. And her stomach was grumbling for more food, but for a specific type of sandwich that she did not have all of the ingredients for.

Getting off the couch, she made her way to the bedroom. As she entered the bedroom, she placed the phone on the side table, and walked over to the closet to pull out a pair of jeans and a sweater. Stripping off her current clothes and tossing them onto the bed, she threw on the jeans and the sweater to prepare her for the cold weather outside her front door. Pulling on the boots, her attention was shifted to the sound of someone pulling up into the driveway. Finishing putting on the boots, she could hear a truck door closing and some light rustling footsteps through the snow ascending the porch steps and ending at the front door. The sound of someone knocking on her front door made her even more confused. Who could be at her house on a Sunday morning, especially in the early morning hours? No one ever comes to her house on Sundays. She picked up her phone and walked to her front door to see who it was that was knocking. The thought of an unknown person at her front door made her nervous and highly uncomfortable. Looking out one of the side windows, she could tell it was a man, but she could not see who it was because of the hoodie jacket that was partially covering his face. She opened the door and was greeted by a familiar face.

"Mathew, what are you doing here?" Ingrid asked, in shock.

"I was wondering if you wanted to go with me to the café."

"Oh, I was actually about to head over there and grab a bite to eat."

"Well, that's good. How do you feel about a date?"

Ingrid looked at him for a moment with a genuine smile on her face and did not know why, but her mind and heart were telling her to say yes. Mathew still stood on her porch in the cool January air waiting on her answer.

"That sounds like fun. So, yes, I would like that."

He smiled big and let out a breath of relief, as if he had been nervous about what her answer might be. Ingrid gathered her purse, keys and jacket; locked the door behind her and followed Mathew to his truck. Mathew led her to the passenger side, opened the door and helped her into the cabin of his truck. Once the door was closed, he made his way to the driver's side, opened the door, climbed in, started the truck and put it in reverse to make his way down her driveway. Turning onto the road, the cabin was filled with silence for a moment, then Ingrid spoke.

"What type of music do you listen to?"

"I listen to a little bit of everything. I would say my favorite type of music is Classic Rock. What's your favorite type of music?"

"I listen to everything as well, but I listen to a lot of jazz music, so jazz is high on my list."

"Very nice. What artists are you into?" Mathew asked with a surprised look on his face—surprised because he never would've thought of her being into jazz music.

"Primarily Rosemary Clooney, Etta James, and Ray LaMontagne. But outside of jazz, I'm a fan of Steppenwolf, Charlie Daniels and Imogen Heap."

"Wow! You certainly do have a wide variety of music tastes."

"Who would you say is your favorite artist or band?"

"I don't have a favorite but I listen to a lot of Air Supply, Steppen-wolf, and Alabama."

"Oh, very nice. I've heard of Air Supply and Alabama, great bands."

"I think so too. I'm sorry though; my stereo is broken right now."

"It's okay. It happens to all of us from time to time."

"True, but this stereo has been broken for over a month. I think a month and a half now."

"What happened to it?"

"Honestly, I don't know. One day it just stopped working. I tried to fix it on my own, but nothing happened. I need to take it to the store to get it fixed, but I keep putting it off."

"Do you enjoy the silence when you are driving?"

"I usually do that too. It gives me some time to focus on everything while I'm heading off to work or if I'm just driving anywhere."

"It seems that we have the same mindset and somewhat similar taste in music."

"Yes, it does. I've yet to meet anyone who has the same mindset as I do. Quite intriguing."

"It's hard to meet others who have this mindset, primarily because others are not letting their thoughts run wild. They hide them inside and never sort through things. It might be because of how they were raised or just how they are in general. Personally, I think you, my mom and I have this mindset."

"Well, my dad is the same way."

"He is?" Mathew asked as his eyes stayed focused on the road.

"Yeah, although physically I'm more like my mom, mentally I'm more like my dad. He takes long drives to go clear his head and just think things through. That, or he just talks to my mom."

"It's nice to know that he has someone he can talk to."

"Yes, it is, and he needs it. It helps him with his everyday life."

"What do your parents do?"

"My dad is a dentist and my mom is an editor with a company but working at home. What do your parents do?"

"My mom is a painter and my dad is a chef."

"Oh wow, that's pretty amazing. You must have had delicious food growing up."

"Yeah, I did. My dad is very talented."

"That's good to hear. Can you cook at all?"

"Yes, I just don't cook often as it's just me."

"Oh, I know how that goes."

"How long have your parents been together?" Ingrid asked and then noticed a change in Mathew's expression.

"They were together for fourteen years. They divorced when I was thirteen."

"Oh, I am so sorry."

"It's okay, you didn't know. What about you?"

"My parents are still married; they've been together for thirty years." She said timidly, trying to say it gently without starting or triggering something that she was not ready for.

"That's great. So, they've been married for thirty years. How old are you?"

"I'm twenty-eight. How old are you?"

"I'm thirty-three. So, we're not too far apart in age."

"Have you ever been married or had kids?" Ingrid asked shyly.

"I've never been married, nor do I have kids. I was engaged, but she broke it off because she fell in love with my best friend."

"Oh, I am so sorry." Ingrid didn't know what to say, so she just stared out the window and didn't say a word.

Mathew took notice of this and started to apologize profusely.

"I am sorry; I hope I didn't make you feel uncomfortable. I was just being honest. I try not to hold anything back when someone asks me questions."

It took Ingrid a couple of minutes before she could answer him.

"There is no reason for you to apologize; I was the one to ask you a question. I tend to be a bit more reserved when others ask me questions, so I was not fully ready to hear that answer."

"Everyone is different when it comes to answering questions. Since you asked me, I'll ask you. Have you ever been married...do you have kids?"

Ingrid took a deep breath. Mathew did not realize that this subject was very touchy for her and she tried to avoid his question, but she knew that she started the conversation and she must answer it in some form so she wouldn't come off rude.

"No, I'm not married," she answered slowly. "And I've never had kids."

Mathew realized how she had answered the question and that she seemed to be a bit bothered by it. Thankfully at that moment, some of the intensity started to fade as the café came into view.

Chapter 6

PULLING INTO THE PARKING LOT, Ingrid felt a sigh of relief flood her entire body, letting her just relax in the seat of the truck. Turning the ignition off and unbuckling his seat belt, Mathew opened the truck door and closed it behind him. Ingrid unbuckled herself from the seat and reached for the door handle, but just before she could open it, it opened for her and Mathew waited with a nice, caring smile. This look gave Ingrid a sense of safety and she smiled back. She jumped down from the truck cabin and her boots met new soft snow. Mathew's free hand reached for one of hers and, hand in hand, they walked to the café.

Walking through the café's front door, they were greeted by the sound of the doorbell. They walked up to the counter and were told to take a seat and someone would be right with them. Walking to a table, they noticed a window that had a beautiful view of the ocean lined with snow and ice. Sitting down at the table, they decided to sit next to each other instead of across from each other. Ingrid let go of his hand and took off her jacket, placed her purse on the back of the chair and pulled her hair away from her face, letting it lay against her back. Mathew watched her, trying to figure her out and couldn't quite put his finger on anything. Ingrid felt this. She looked at Mathew with a little smile on her face. He smiled back. He was about to say something, but he was interrupted before he could say anything.

"Hey, you two. Never thought I would see the day when my two favorite people would be in here together. What can I get for you today?" The man was middle-aged with salt-and-peppered hair and piercing blue eyes. His medium build gave others a sense of safety and comfort.

Mathew looked at Ingrid and motioned for her to order first.

"I will have the sandwich-of-the-day with a cup of tea."

"Do you want green tea or what type would you like?"

"Green tea will be just fine. Thank you, Hans."

The man then turned his attention to Mathew to take his order.

"I'll have the potato soup if you have it. If not, then I'll have the soup-of-the- day."

"What will you have to drink?"

"Hot, green tea will be good. Thank you."

The man walked toward the kitchen with their order.

Mathew took his eyes off the water and placed them on Ingrid.

"What's on your mind?" He asked her while studying her face.

"I am just a little uncomfortable. It's been a while since I've been on a date."

"How long?"

"At least three years."

"Oh wow, it *has* been a while for you."

"How long has it been for you?"

For a moment Mathew just looked at her, thinking about the question and trying to figure out why he was so drawn to her.

"It's been five years for me," he finally said.

"Looks like we have more in common than we thought" Ingrid murmured shyly.

Mathew smiled and placed his hand on top of hers. Ingrid looked down at his hand then back up to notice his lingering gaze. It was not a look that she had seen before. It was a different look, one that she had only read about or seen in the movies. It seemed to be the look of love. But she was still unsure. She was thinking she might be misinterpreting what she was reading. Here she was, doing what she does best, suddenly just thinking that he might be in love with her, but then her mind would flip a switch and tell that she was wrong from the beginning and that no one would fall in love with her.

While Ingrid was having this war inside her mind, Mathew was having his own little war inside his mind. He was feeling something for her, but just like her, his mind was telling him that she would never love him. He, too, was broken and felt not worthy. There was a secret that he shared with very few people: He also was bipolar. Just like Ingrid, he dealt with his highs and lows. He dealt with his mind trying to rule his thoughts and body, but each day he fought this mind-menace; with all of his strength, he fought it. He would never admit to anyone—even to himself—that he wished he could give into the war inside his mind, but he pushed himself to keep on fighting, to keep getting stronger and not let the disorder control him or his life.

While they both were smiling, holding hands and peering into each others' eyes, their attention was caught by the waiter who cheerfully placed their plates of food in front of them and their cups of tea to the side, before walking back to the kitchen.

They both let go of each other's hands and turned to the food. Ingrid took a bite of her sandwich and looked over at Mathew eating his soup.

"How does the soup taste?" she asked between bites.

"It tastes very good; they did have the potato soup."

Ingrid tried to hold back a good-natured chuckle, but was unable to. "I'm happy that you are so elated to have the potato soup."

"Oh, yes, I am."

"Is it your favorite?"

"Very much so. I do have a few other favorites."

"Oh, and what others do you enjoy?"

"Lamb stew and goulash. I know a lot of people don't like goulash, but I love it."

"Goulash is very good. It's been a while since I've had it. I think the last time I had it was in high school when my grandma came over for the holidays."

"It has been a while since I've had it too. So...I'm curious about something," he said as he raised a spoonful of soup to his lips. "What do you think of me right now? What is your impression of me?" He took a bite and looked calm on the outside like a serene pond, but on the inside, he was a nervous wreck, a tempestuous sea. He couldn't believe that he asked that question to her, to a person he was very much interested in. Ingrid had taken a bite of the sandwich when he had asked her this question. She didn't know how to answer, the feelings percolating in her for him were very strong and something that she had never had before. While she thoughtfully chewed on the sandwich, she was tried to come up with the best answer to give him. Once she finished the bite, she grabbed the tea, took a sip, and then spoke.

"I like you and it's very unique and rare to fall for someone this soon."

She took another bite of her sandwich, then her mind registered what she had said and at that moment she got worried. She had confessed her feelings to a man that she just met! As she just stared at her sandwich and continued to chew, she felt Mathew's eyes on her. And that feeling was accurate. Mathew had stopped from taking a bite of his soup and looked at her when she had admitted that.

"How do you feel about me?"

Ingrid asked while she focused intently on her sandwich. Her heart raced faster, and her palms were starting to clam up. She was afraid his answer might hurt. But what happened next took her by surprise.

"From the first moment I saw you, I was enthralled by you. There was something that captured my attention, as if you were to be a significant part of my life."

The only sound after that moment was the sound of them chewing their food. Neither of them said a word for at least five minutes as they focused fixedly on their meals. The silence was then broken by the waiter approaching their table.

"How is everything?" he asked the two of them.

"It tastes delicious." Ingrid said with a smile on her face.

"I agree; this is great. Thank Henrik for cooking the food," Mathew said to the waiter.

"I will certainly do that."

The waiter walked away and they locked eyes, smiling warmly.

This is silly, Ingrid thought to herself, *we are both adults—not two teenagers going through puberty.*

"What are your plans for the week?" Mathew asked her as he took another bite of his soup.

"I have work at the ranch all week, and then I don't know what else. What do you have going on for you?"

"This week I'm going to Ireland. I'm leaving tomorrow."

"Oh, what are you doing over there?"

"I'm visiting family that I haven't seen in two years."

"It's definitely time to see them then."

"Very much so."

The waiter returned with the check, silently placed it on the table, and walked away.

"What time do you leave?"

"I leave very early; the flight is at 6 AM."

"What part of Ireland are you going to? I lived in Ireland when I was younger."

"Really? What area? I'm going to a small town south of Dublin."

"Never been to Dublin. But I lived in Shannon for a few years. In fact, my younger brother Eli was born there."

"Such a great place, do you miss it?"

"Yes and no. I love that country but this is my favorite place."

"This country is a pretty amazing place too."

Mathew reached for his wallet just as Ingrid reached for her wallet that was in her purse. He stopped her from paying the meal. "No need to do that. I'm paying. I did, after all, ask you on this date, didn't I?" He said with a sweet smile.

She was taken aback by it and didn't know how to deal with it. She had never had anyone pay for her meal. She had been so independent for so long and that to see another person do this made her feel strange—like she had lost a little bit of her independence. But she didn't say anything, for she didn't want to appear rude and ungrateful.

After Mathew paid for their meals, he asked what her plans were for the rest of the day. She explained that she would take a nap and then just relax for the rest of the day so she would have plenty of energy for the work week. He listened and was curious about why she needed to relax in order to have energy. To him, she seemed athletic and energetic already. He didn't want to pry further into that area, so once she was finished talking, he just blurted out, "Do you want to go for a ride?"

Well, this is random, she thought, but she thought about it for a second and knew that she shouldn't lock herself up in her home 24/7.

"That would be nice."

"Great! I have an area that I want to show you. You will love it."

"I'm looking forward to seeing it."

They gathered up all of their belongings from the café, then climbed back into the truck. The truck heater began to warm the entire cabin, which warmed them both up from the cold air that had been dancing around them. Ingrid rubbed her hands together and blew into them. Mathew did the same. Sitting in the parking lot, letting the truck and themselves warm up, they sat there in silence. Only the sounds of their breathing and the heater filled the cabin.

Soon enough, Mathew's hands were warm and he began to pull out of the parking lot. Instead of going the usual way, which led them back to each of their respective homes, he turned down the opposite way and started to drive towards the place he mentioned. The entire time, Ingrid stared out the window and didn't say a word. Her thoughts were keeping her preoccupied: the thoughts of her warm bed, of hiding away, of not going to work tomorrow. She could tell the depression was starting to make its home inside her mind again, and she was trying to fight it. On the outside, she looked calm; in fact, it looked like she was at peace and just focused on the snow and the rest of the scenery outside her window. Even though her eyes seemed to be focused on the snow, she was focusing mentally on the images in her mind. Mathew looked over to look at Ingrid to see if she was okay. It looked like she was okay, but his thoughts started to run wild. *Oh no*, he thought. *She's having a horrible time; she's not enjoying this.*

His thoughts ran similarly to hers; he had his ups and his downs. But his downs always automatically added to thoughts of him being worthless, thinking everything he was doing was wrong and he was no fun at all. Such thoughts were deadly for him. Such thoughts have brought him to moments of his life—just like Ingrid's—like suicide. He had attempted several times and ended up in the hospital each time, saved somehow. He never knew what was going on, but he believed that there was someone looking out for him.

It seemed like they had been going down the road for hours, but it had only been twenty minutes. It was the thick snow-covered roads that made it seem like it had been a long time. Looking around to see where they were, Mathew realized that they were not far from the destination.

"We're almost there."

This snapped Ingrid out of the trance-like state, and her thoughts disappeared for that moment.

"What? Oh, okay. Where is this place?"

"It's a few more minutes, located near the edge of town."

"Near the ocean?"

"Yes, it is."

Ingrid started to think about where they were going. She had no clue where she was. Everything was covered by snow and all the landmarks were hidden from view.

Soon, she could see something pointy and peering out of the distance. She could see a roof come into view and realized where she was. They were approaching the church that sat next to the ocean. Mathew pulled up near the church, parked the truck, turned it off, turned to Ingrid and motioned her out of the truck to follow him. They headed down the path towards the church and both paid attention to the surroundings and enjoyed the sweet gentle kisses of the wind on their cheeks. Mathew reached for Ingrid's hand and guided her off the main path, towards another

52

path that did not go near the church. Soon enough, she realized they were walking towards the shores of the ocean. Mathew looked over at her and noticed she seemed cold, even with her jacket on.

"Are you doing okay?"

"Yeah, I'm okay."

"You seem to be cold."

"Oh, no, I'm fine. My face just gets flushed in cool weather. It's in my genetics."

"Oh, are you originally from Iceland?"

"I was born and raised here—not in this town of course, but my dad is from the United Kingdom and my mom is from Sweden."

"What brought them all the way out here?"

"My dad was attending college to be a dentist and my mom was just starting as an editor at the company that she's been with for over twenty-five years. My dad has been a dentist for over twenty years now."

"That is truly impressive. Is your dad a good dentist?"

Ingrid slipped and fell on her butt, making her burst out laughing.

"Are you okay?" Mathew asked, laughing with her.

"Yes." She said, extending her arms and hands out towards him, so he could help her up from the snow. "But now my pants are wet." She continued to laugh.

Mathew helped her up and they continued walking.

"But to answer your question, yes...my dad is a very good dentist. I remember him doing my braces, teeth cleanings and fillings growing up, and he was gentle. Most people look at him and assume he would hurt them, but he is very gentle."

"Why would people assume he would hurt them?"

"My dad is very big guy and the sight of him tends to be a bit intimidating to others."

"How big of a guy is he?"

"6 ' 2."

"Wow! Tall guy." Mathew said.

"Oh yeah, he's tall and has a burly build, so he looks intimidating. To me, though, he's just a big teddy bear."

Mathew started laughing again.

"I wonder how he would feel if I ever saw him and called him Teddy Bear."

Ingrid laughed.

"I don't know what would happen, but that would be funny to watch. I wouldn't be able to keep a straight face if you ever did that."

In high spirits, they both continued the walk and continued to laugh. Neither of them was aware that they were getting closer to the destination. They were too focused on one another and weren't paying attention to the surroundings. Mathew stopped and noticed where they were.

"Over here…"

Ingrid followed him and when he stopped, so did she.

"Now look out into the ocean. What do you see?"

Ingrid looked in the direction he pointed at and noticed something moving in the distance. She focused her eyes and realized it was an animal. Soon she could see what kind. It was a penguin, floating on a big patch of ice with a few more following it!

"That is so beautiful. I've never seen a penguin this close before—only on TV."

Mathew marveled at the penguin, watching it waddle around on the patch of ice. He took notice that the penguin would every so often consider the cold grey sea, as if it was looking for someone. Moments later, another penguin emerged from the water and scooted onto the ice.

Ingrid looked from the penguins over to Mathew who had walked up a few steps on the shore. Her eyes darted back and forth between him and the penguin, trying to surmise the connection, but she couldn't figure it out. Now her mind was racing, just like his mind was before when they were in the truck. *What was he thinking? Is he okay? Why is he fascinated by this penguin?* These thoughts were now plaguing her mind. Meanwhile, inside Mathew's mind, it was calm as the cold grey sea below his feet. The sight of the sea soothed him. The penguin had been the first one he had ever seen up close; he could tell it was the same penguin because of a certain white spot under its eye. That particular penguin had come ashore one day when Mathew was there, and sat next to him. They had bonded—a rarity—but there was something about Mathew that the penguin sensed…that he was a kind human being who meant him no harm. The penguin sensed something was wrong with his friend, so whenever he saw Mathew, he would waddle up to the shore to sit with him. This day the penguin noticed his friend and an unknown person. The penguin jumped off the patch of ice, and began to swim to the shore. Mathew just continued to stare out into the ocean while Ingrid was looking for the penguin and wondering what was going on. Soon the penguin emerged from the sea, walked onto the shore, and up to his friend. Mathew looked down at the penguin and greeted him as if he were an old friend. Ingrid was surprised by all of this; she had no clue as to what was going on. She just watched them both sit down on the shore and just relax together as if they were childhood friends.

Mathew talked to the penguin. The penguin looked back at him as if he understood what he was saying to him. Mathew then looked over at Ingrid with a smile on his face.

"Ingrid, this is Pebble. He has been out here for quite some time and he came up to me one day when I was sitting on the shore. We've become good friends. I wanted you two to meet each other." Ingrid looked at Mathew with a smile and turned to the penguin.

"Hello, Pebble," she said, smiling at him.

Pebble got up from where he was sitting and waddled over to her slowly. He looked at her, studied her face and body (as all penguins do—they are smart). Once he stopped studying her, he walked closer then stopped. He looked down, found the loveliest stone he could find, picked it up and carried the stone over to her. She held out her hand, and he placed the stone in her hand.

Mathew watched this happen. He was in shock. He had never known Pebble to do that before. Once, Mathew had brought a friend with him and Pebble never went near the girl. He just stayed close to Mathew the entire time. The girl tried to get

Pebble's attention, but for some reason he just did not like her. Mathew did not know why until weeks later, when he realized that this friend of his was toxic and was worsening his mental health.

But Mathew didn't want to lose a friend just because she was not thinking about him. He didn't want to get rid of her because he had very few friends. In fact, he could count on one hand how many friends he had. Ultimately, those two stopped talking and he had not seen her since that day.

Pebble got closer to Ingrid and gave her the penguin-version-of-a-hug, then waddled back to Mathew. Ingrid never had this happen to her before; she was excited. Pebble sat next to Mathew once again, and Ingrid joined them by sitting on the other side of Mathew. All three of them sat there in silence, staring out into the sea. Suddenly, Ingrid felt something on her hand. She looked down to see Mathew's hand holding hers and looked up at him with a smile. He smiled back. This was the first time in a long time that she enjoyed holding hands with someone, and it did not terrify her at all. Their eyes met and held for a moment. There is a adage that says the eyes are the windows to the soul. That is very much true. It seemed like Mathew could see into her soul and see everything that she felt at that moment, what her heart was feeling, what she was dealing with. Ingrid had never witnessed this herself, but she had heard of others knowing when they found the love of their lives. She felt as though she was seeing every intimate part of his soul and his heart—the parts he kept hidden from everyone else. She also felt like she had seen what he had been going through. This frightened her, and yet it seemed to feel right. They did not realize that Pebble had left and had gone back to the floating ice patch. But when they looked down, they realized that Pebble had left each of them two stones at their feet.

Mathew stood up and extended his hands to Ingrid so she could grab onto him and he could pull her up. Walking hand in hand back to the trail path, Mathew looked back to see Pebble with another penguin—one that turned out to be a girl. Mathew smiled and proceeded up the trail with Ingrid. Walking back, they were both silent, just as they were on the shore. Soon they were back on the trail that led to the church, but instead of going to the church, they headed back to the truck. The snow had begun to fall again, which did not bother either one of them. The snowflakes landed in Ingrid's red wavy hair and onto Mathew's hoodie jacket. It wasn't long before they reached the truck. Mathew unlocked the doors and helped Ingrid get in before getting himself in. Starting up the truck, Mathew looked over to see Ingrid warming her hands, just like she had done before. He smiled and got on the road heading back toward the town. Both of their minds were calm; they were very much enjoying the Sunday morning, spending it together. Mathew was looking forward to doing this more, and Ingrid was thinking the same thing. She was starting to think that something permanent would come out of this. As she looked out the window, she had a slight smile on her face, then suddenly shifted her attention when she felt Mathew's hand again on hers. They looked at each other and smiled. He turned his eyes back to the road and the entire ride back was in silence. This did not bother either one of them. In fact, the silence seemed to just let their energies and body language do the talking for them. It would be nearly forty-five minutes till they would arrive at Ingrid's home. Until then, the silence filled the cabin. Ingrid's eyes locked onto the scenery that was outside her window. The snow seemed brighter, although it was impossible, for the sun was hiding behind the thick clouds and playing peek-a-boo with the snow below. Nevertheless, the snow seemed brighter and the day seemed to be going quite well, at least to her. With her morning starting off quite depressing, it was nearing noon, and it was as if the day was going by slowly for her so she could enjoy the morning with him, and be able to go on a date with a man who was genuine and had his own ways of thinking, and it seemed like he couldn't hurt a fly.

As he drove, Mathew would look over to Ingrid every so often to see if she was okay. And each time he looked, he saw the same scene over and over: Her contentedly watching the snow falling, creating a high wall. The snow crunched underneath the tires and the sound of this relaxed Mathew as he continued to drive down the road.

Soon enough, the town came into view and they passed through the town, passing the school, the bank and a few stores. Soon they were passing by the road to get to the café, and that meant they would soon be at her house. Mathew didn't want the day to end, but he knew she needed to get ready for the week at work and he needed to finish packing for his trip to Ireland the next day. Over in the passenger seat, Ingrid was thinking the same thing. Her eyes were still hooked on the snow falling outside;

inside her mind, however, she was wishing he would slow down his driving and take his time so they could keep holding hands and just spend more time together. Without realizing it, Mathew had indeed slowed down and tried to savor the moment, because it would be a while till he would see her again.

Up ahead, he could see the driveway that led to her house and prepared to make the turn. Ingrid's ears perked up when she heard the turn signal click on. A mixture of dread and excitement rushed over her body. She didn't want him to take her home, yet she wanted to say home, catch up on her sleep, and just relax for the day. She felt like her cozy bed was waiting for her. His own sensation of wanting to spend more time with her rushed over him, waterfall-like. Pulling into the long driveway, Ingrid locked her eyes on the house. The truck came to a stop. Mathew turned it off, unbuckled and jumped down, and walked around the front of the truck. Ingrid was gathering her purse, unbuckling and reaching for the door handle. As she began to open the door, the door jerked open on her and she began to tumble out of the truck. Mathew grabbed her in time and she didn't fall onto the snow.

"Got you." He said as he laughed softly and Ingrid got herself steady on the snow. Mathew closed the truck door, took hold of one of her hands and began to walk towards the front door of her home. Both were a bit sad that this had to end, but both knew that they would see each other in a week or so. Walking up the porch steps, the silence was then silenced by the sound of Mathew's voice.

"I had a great time today. I hope we can do this again when I get back."

"I enjoyed this morning; certainly I would like to see you again. You'll be back in a week, right?"

"Correct. If I have any time while I'm over there, I'll give you a call and check up on you."

"If you can, then do so, but if you are unable to, then it is okay, because it's only a week."

She even knew that it would be awkward for him to be gone for a while. Just thinking this, she was wondering why she felt this way. She was very much interested in Mathew; he seemed to be pretty much perfect, but she didn't want to attach herself too early. She didn't want to seem desperate. Indeed, she wanted to be in a relationship; she just didn't want to ruin this...whatever it might be between them.

"Thank you for a great date. I'm looking forward to seeing you again. I'm going to go inside. Hope you have a safe flight to Ireland tomorrow."

"Very much welcome. It was an honor to go on a date with you. I hope you have a nice, relaxing day, and I'll let you know when I land."

"That sounds good to me."

Ingrid reached for her keys in the purse, pulled them out and placed the key into the door to unlock it. Mathew watched her as she stepped inside, while he still stood on her porch.

"Have a nice rest of your day," she said to him.

"You too, Dear."

He walked back to his truck, started it up again and drove down the driveway, turning to head to his house.

Ingrid closed the door, locked it, took off her jacket and put it away on the back of the chair in the hallway. There she removed her boots and walked to her bedroom, with her phone in her hand, and checked her messages. She noticed that she missed a message from her brother.

"Made it!" the message said.

Seeing it gave her some relief about her brother's safety. She replied to him and told him to have a good semester, and that he is always welcome at her house. Her brother replied, and once she read it, she sat the phone down on the side table and laid down for a nap.

Chapter 7

INGRID WOKE UP three hours later, looking at her phone to see what time it was. She knew that she couldn't stay in bed all day; she would not be able to get sleep if she did. She left her bedroom and then went to the kitchen. She saw the sink filled with the dishes from her brother's visit. Walking to the sink, she sat the phone down on the table and then turned on the faucet, grabbed a sponge and began washing the dishes. Then she took a dry dishtowel and dried each one by hand and placed them in the cabinets and drawers. Drying off her own hands, Ingrid looked around the kitchen to see if there was anything else that she needed to do. Once she realized that there was nothing left to do, she grabbed her phone and left the room.

Venturing down the hallway, Ingrid looked around to see what she could do with her free time. *I could read a book*, she thought to herself. *Or I could just watch another movie.* She stopped in front of her library door, opened it and walked in. Closing the door behind her, her eyes began to scan the shelves of her books. Her eyes found the titles *Chronicles of Narnia*, *Peter Pan*, *Persuasion*, among many others. Then she scanned the biography books of her favorite authors, artists and philosophers. Finally settling on a book, she walked to the location it was in. Pulling the book from the shelf, she let her fingers trace the title. *The Lady of the Lake*, it read. A sense of relief rushed over her. A sense of calm rippled through her skin, entered her body, and then left as quickly as it had entered. She walked over to the cushioned chair, let it recline, and then settled into the book. The first few lines began:

> *"Harp of the North! That mouldering long hast hung*
> *On the witch-elm that shades Saint Fillan's spring,*
> *And down the fitful breeze thy numbers flung,*
> *Till envious ivy did around thee cling.*
> *Muffling with verdant ringlet every string,*
> *O minstrel harp, still must thine accents sleep?"*

Within seconds, it seemed to her that the words on the page blurred and images played inside her mind, creating a movie scene that was meant only for her to see, and no one else. As she continued to read, the snow outside continued to fall and create a thicker coat for the world outside her window. Only after an hour of reading, Ingrid heard something come up the driveway. Getting out of the chair, she made her way to the window and looked outside to see a familiar vehicle parking in her driveway. Setting the book down, Ingrid opened the door of the library, walked out and closed it behind her. She made her way to the front door, unlocked it and opened it up to see her father standing on her front porch. He was bundled up in a jacket that seemed to make him appear bigger than he was.

"Dad!" Ingrid said in a surprised tone. "Come in."

Her dad walked into the house, and she closed and locked the door behind them. Her dad took off his snowy jacket and hung it in the nearby closet. His build was between athletic and burly, and his red hair was full and thick just like his short beard; and like his son, Arthur had green eyes. They were very handsome; his eyes were like emeralds of the sea. Standing in front of his daughter, a sense of worry settled over him. Even though Ingrid had a smile on her face, her dad could tell that there was something wrong with his daughter. He had that same expression when he was her age. And even now, as he was heading into his fifties, he occasionally had that same look. His wife had seen the look a million times: the look of constant fear, always being tired, putting on a façade. Nothing new. Arthur did not like the fact that he saw the same expression on his daughter's face. Without hesitation, he grabbed Ingrid and hugged her. Burying her face into his chest, she muffled something.

"What was that, Dear?"

"Why are you here, Dad?"

"I came to check on you. I am worried about you."

"You didn't have to come all the way out here."

"Yes, I did."

Ingrid again buried her face into his chest and didn't move. She muffled a thank you, and her dad kissed the top of her head. After a few moments of them hugging in front of the door, they both let go.

"You do realize that I have to work tomorrow." Ingrid said as she looked at her dad.

"Yes, I know. And that is okay."

"What will you do while I'm at work?"

"I'll find something to do. Don't worry."

"Okay," she said as she started down the hallway.

"Do you want tea?"

"Yeah, that'll be great. I haven't had the chance to get warmed up today with a cup of tea."

Ingrid walked to the kitchen and began to make her dad a cup of tea. She grabbed the yellow mug and poured boiling water into it. As she was steeping the tea, her dad walked into the kitchen and just looked at her.

Arthur seemed to be a tough guy, but he was a very sensitive man. The thought of his own child dealing with the same mental illness terrified him. And when Ingrid was diagnosed, his fear had become reality. Arthur had no clue how to handle it from a new view. His whole life, he had dealt with the mental illness. He had his highs and his lows. The lows were deadly, just like they were deadly for Ingrid. In college, when he had just begun dating Isobel (now his wife), he had a very low moment. He grabbed the gun that his father had given him for his birthday, got in his truck, and drove off to a well-wooded area that was at least forty minutes away from the school. Sitting in his truck, he turned up the stereo and placed the gun to his temple. He pulled the trigger, but nothing happened. He cried for what seemed to be hours on end. He looked inside the gun to find that there were no bullets in it. His father had placed all the bullets inside a container, and placed the container inside the box he had given to Arthur. Now sitting in his truck with an unloaded gun, he was exhausted with anguish and had started to doze off, but the sound of footsteps outside his truck had caught him off guard. Putting the gun in the compartment, he looked to see who it was. It was the runners; they were getting their training down. Once they were out of sight and out of his truck's way, he made his way back onto the main road and headed back to the campus.

This memory played in his head as he stared at his daughter. She smiled and then he smiled. Pulling the tea bag out of the mug, she tossed the bag into the sink and handed the mug to her dad. He nodded a thank you and they headed to the living room. They sat in the living room while her dad drank the tea, and they watched some classic films together. She had soon realized it was 10 o'clock at night, so they turned the television off and went to their respective rooms—but not before her dad gave her a kiss on the forehead. Both bedroom doors closed. Crawling into bed, Ingrid set her alarm so that she could get up early and eat breakfast before work. Her head hit the pillow, but before her eyes shut, she could already hear her dad snoring from the down the hall. Then she fell asleep.

Chapter 8

WAKING UP, Ingrid felt strange. She had woken up crying, consumed with dread. Her body fought against her. She tried to get out of bed, but her mind was telling her to go back to sleep. Still crying, she pulled on her clothes and boots, and she made her way down the hall. The tears had stopped, but the gnawing feeling was still there. Trying to fight it, her body became weak. Every step she took, her thighs felt like they weighed a hundred pounds each. Trying not to awaken her dad, she slowly walked past the guest bedroom door and made her way into the kitchen. Grabbing the tea kettle, she filled it up, placed it on the stove and brought the water to a boil. She placed a tea bag in her mug and filled it. Standing in the middle of the kitchen, holding the mug with both hands, a tear rolled down her face.

"Bloody ridiculous!" Ingrid said out loud, but not loud enough for her father to hear her. Her head was hurting and the only place she wanted to be was in her bed.

Suddenly she heard the guest bedroom door open and the sound of grunting made its way up to the kitchen. Before long, he stood in the kitchen with her and was fumbling around, bumping into everything in sight. As Ingrid watched this, she didn't know what to do. *Maybe he's still trying to wake up*, she thought to herself. As she watched her dad, she noticed he had gotten a mug and tea bag, then filled the mug with the boiling water.

"Good morning, Dad," she said softly.

"Good morning, Dear," he replied while grumbling.

"How did you sleep?" Ingrid asked.

"Shitty," he said while staring into the mug. He gave Ingrid a kiss on the head and walked out of the kitchen. "I'm heading back to bed. Have a good day at work."

Ingrid finished her cup of tea, placed the mug into the sink, walked to the bathroom and splashed water onto her face to cool it after shedding so many tears. As she walked out of the house, she grabbed her jacket, keys, purse, and yelled goodbye to her dad.

The fresh morning air greeted her as if she were a long-lost relative. Walking to the truck, she looked back at the house and noticed her dad standing at the window waving. She waved good-bye and got into her truck. The drive to work was typical: the music played, the heater warmed her up, and snow was covering everything around her. Once she pulled up the driveway to the ranch, she noticed her boss had already begun to start feeding the horses. Pulling into her normal parking spot, she turned the truck off and made her way out to head over to her boss.

Back at Ingrid's house, Arthur sat on the edge of the bed staring into his empty hands. A tear rolled down his face and dropped on top of his hand. Slowly standing up, he slipped his feet into his shoes, grumbled then walked out of the bedroom. As he approached the front door, he grabbed his keys and coat and was then greeted by the fresh, cool air. He just breathed it in and looked around the front yard of her house, then finally decided to close the front door. As he walked down the steps, he twirled his keys in his fingers letting them make a jingling sound. He approached his truck and unlocked it, then jumped inside.

The entire time he did this, he had a stoic look upon his face, as if he was numb from everything, numb to all emotions, numb to the environment that was around him. Turning on the truck, he let out a big sigh and began to drive down the driveway. He didn't even bother putting on his seatbelt—he just drove. His mind was numb and free of thoughts.

The road around him shined brightly with the sun rays beaming down on the snow. The glistening snow tried to blind him, tried to make him slow down, but to no avail. He kept going. Soon, he found a secluded place in the middle of nowhere outside of the town. He stopped where he was and just looked at the dashboard in front of him. Placed on the dashboard was the gun his father had given him. Staring at the gun, he began to cry. The tears fell so fast and hard, but he did not care. He just let them fall. Engulfed by everything and nothing all at once, the numb feeling filled his mind.

Reaching for the gun, he looked around. No one, there was no one for miles. With this, he was happy—happy that no one could stop him, happy that he could finally get rid of the pain. He raised the gun to his temple, cocked the gun, and pulled the trigger.

Chapter 9

IT WAS 6 O'CLOCK when Ingrid got back home from the ranch. As she pulled up to the house, she noticed something was wrong. There were three police cars in her driveway and all the officers were standing and talking. When she pulled up into her spot, she was hesitant to even get out. In the pit of her stomach, she knew something was wrong.

Turning the truck off, she slowly got out and proceeded to walk towards the cops.

"Hello, everyone," she said as she looked at each one of them.

They all looked at her and took off their hats.

"Hello, Ingrid. May we go inside for a moment?" one of the officers asked, his face shadowed by seriousness.

"Sure," she said as she noticed her dad's vehicle gone.

The police officers and Ingrid went inside and she led them toward the living room. As they passed the guest bedroom, the youngest police officer who looked to be in his mid-twenties asked, "What is in this room?"

Ingrid looked at the door he motioned towards.

"Oh, that's the guest bedroom. I currently have a visitor."

"Who would that be, if you don't mind my asking?" the young officer asked.

"My dad. He must be out doing something."

She turned down the hallway to the living room and motioned for the officers to take a seat.

The young officer grabbed a chair and sat Ingrid down in it. With this happening, she became confused.

"May I ask what is going on, officers?"

The young officer sighed, and one of the senior officers spoke.

"Miss Ingrid, I regret to inform you that we've found your dad." His salt and peppered moustache twitched as he said these words.

"What..." She began to speak, but then it registered in her mind. Her face went pale, her body began to shake, and she buried her face in her hands and began to cry.

All the officers lowered their heads and closed their eyes as to give a moment of silence before the younger one spoke.

"Miss Ingrid, I hate to ask, but may I look inside the guest bedroom for any clues?"

Through the tears, Ingrid muffled a yes. He made his way to the room, opened the door and began to look around. Another officer made his way toward the guest room. The officer with salt and peppered hair finally spoke, breaking the lingering silence.

"Ingrid, when was the last time you saw your dad?"

One of the officers came back into the room and stood by the chair where Ingrid sat. Through the tears running down her face, she spoke with gasping breathing, "I saw him this morning before I went to work."

"Did anything look out of place?"

"No," she said, shaking her head as she sobbed.

The young officer came out of the guest bedroom, darted his eyes at the older officer, and cleared his throat, grabbing the attention of the officer. The older officer looked in the direction of the young officer who was now motioning him to come over.

"Excuse me, Miss Ingrid," the senior officer said. He told the other officer in the room to stay with her for a moment, then proceeded down the hallway to the young officer.

"What is it, Alvar?" the officer asked as his eyes strained to look in the bedroom.

"Sir, you need to come look at this," Alvar said. "It's a suicide note."

The older officer looked apprehensive. The last time he had read a suicide note was when his younger sister committed suicide over fifteen years prior. That note had been haunting his nightmares since then.

"Daniel, Sir, do you want to see it?" Alvar asked.

"Yes, show me where it is" Daniel said, after a moment of hesitation.

Both officers went into the room and Daniel immediately started scanning the room for anything else.

"Here it is, Sir," Alvar said as he pointed to it.

Officer Daniel walked over and saw that it was only one page and yet very intimate. Putting on gloves, Daniel's breathing quickened and he started shaking. Removing the letter from the desk, Officer Daniel began to read the note.

Isobel, Ingrid, and Eli;

The words in my head cannot escape through my lips. The pain in my heart cannot escape either. The thoughts that have been racing through my mind more and more, have consumed me. They have consumed me to the point of extinction. The pain in my heart has gotten worse, the feeling of being alone has become more of a reality. I know that I can feel and see the love from all of you, yet this battle inside me seems to have overtaken me more and more each day.

Isobel, I love you very much, my darling. Ingrid, my darling daughter, please don't let the battle inside you consume you as it has done to me. Eli, my son, you will be an amazing man, teacher, husband, and father one day. Do not let that fire inside you grow cold.

I am sorry to all of you, but I wish to end this pain, end these thoughts, end these endless mornings of being so numb and feeling as if I am not contributing anything to myself or the world.

Sorry.

Dad

Officer Alvar stood in the doorway as office Daniel stared at the letter with a stunned expression.

"Sir?" Officer Alvar asked.

Nothing—Officer Daniel said nothing. He didn't know what to say. Slowly, Officer Daniel placed the letter into a bag that he had pulled out from his jacket. Zipping the bag, he walked down the hallway with Officer Alvar to the living room where the third officer and Ingrid stood.

"Miss Ingrid, will you be okay?" Officer Daniel asked.

While sniffling and still sobbing, Ingrid kept her head down and softly spoke, "yes, I... I just need to call my family."

"Would you like one of my officers to stay with you?"

"No, it isn't necessary."

"If you need anything, anything at all, just give me a call," Officer Daniel said, as he gave her his direct extension.

The officers left the house, leaving Ingrid all alone in the living room. Tears kept falling, and she was trying to catch her breath. Wiping away the tears as new ones formed, Ingrid looked around for her phone. Standing up, she slowly wrapped herself with a blanket from the couch, and began to look for her phone. Noticing her purse on the floor, she walked to it and started rummaging through it. Finally finding the phone, she stared at it for what seemed hours but had only been a few minutes. She began dialing, pressed the call button, and placed it to her ear.

Ring! Ring!

"Hello?"

Ingrid could not contain herself. The tears were beginning to drown her in a sea of sorrow, and her breathing became even more erratic.

"Hello?" the voice on the other end said.

"H-hello." Ingrid finally said as she slowed her breathing down even though the tears would not subside.

"May I help you?"

"Mum, it's me, Ingrid."

"Ingrid! Why are you calling me at work? Is something wrong?"

"Yes, Mum, Da-" Ingrid cried louder.

"What is it, Dear?"

"D-dad, is gone."

"What do you mean, Honey?"

"He…he committed suicide."

Ingrid continued crying as her mom got quiet. For the longest time, Isobel, her mother, did not know what to say. She just stared blankly ahead of her as the phone was pressed to her ear and her mouth was slightly open.

"Wa-wait, what? When did this happen?" Isobel stammered. She was trying to figure out if all of this was real, if the man she loved so much was truly gone. Isobel did not and could not accept the fact that her husband was gone.

"It was while I was at work today. When I got home, there were officers here and they told me that they had found him." Ingrid said with labored breathing; tears streaming down her face.

Unsettling quiet—the phone was quiet again.

"Mum?" Ingrid said softly. Suddenly she heard her mom burst into crying and tried to keep herself together, but it was impossible. The man she loved, the man she built a life with was now gone.

Now, they both were crying uncontrollably and that's all they could do. Not a single word escaped from either of their mouths, just the sound of crying escaped. After being on the phone with one another and crying, they made plans to meet up within a day "or two to make funeral arrangements, and then said their good-byes.

Ingrid heard the phone click, realizing that she was no longer on the phone with her mom. She held the phone in her hands, eyes closed, and was just hoping all of this was a dream, hoping that this was just an elaborate prank that her father had devised. But in her mind, she knew that she would never get to see her dad ever again, never get to talk to him again, and never go on those spontaneous trips to the libraries and learn more about him. Instead, the next time she would see him was going to be dressed in his suit in a coffin. She wasn't ready. But then again, who is ever ready for the death of a loved one?

Ingrid placed her phone on the coffee table in front of her, got up to go to the kitchen to make a cup of tea, then brought it back to the living room. The entire time she cried an immensity of tears. Ingrid had placed her cup on the table, turned on the television, laid down on the blanket-covered couch, and just cried. She wanted it all to just be a dream; she wanted this nightmare to be gone and wished it had never occurred. The man who was her own flesh and blood—the one that she was so close to and shared so many memories with—was gone.

As the television screen became blurry, her tears started to put her into a sleep state, and suddenly she had fallen asleep.

Chapter 10

THE AIR WAS NOT COLD, yet Ingrid's breath appeared in the air in front of her, and the snow on the ground seemed to be fresh and new. The dead trees were all around her and seemed to have created a path for her through the snow and forest. Looking behind her, Ingrid could see that it was the same behind her as it was before her. She took one step forward and heard something rustling around her, as if it were trying to get her attention but not startle her away. Taking another step, the rustling sound got louder and closer.

"Hello?" Ingrid shouted.

No answer.

"Hello?!" shouting again.

Yet again, no answer. Without hesitating, Ingrid continued down the snowy path and looked around. She was curious as to how she was not cold, because it was winter, and there was fresh snow on the ground. Her mind started wandering as she continued walking. As she got further on the path, she could see a figure up ahead. Unable to make out who it was, Ingrid decided to stay where she was, then proceeded to call out.

"Hello? Are you okay?"

The figure was covered by a cloak, so Ingrid was unable to see whether the person was peering at her.

"If you are hurt, I can help you!" Ingrid yelled to the figure.

At this point, the figure budged. Stepping onto the path, the figure motioned Ingrid to follow and not say a word. Then the figure started slowly walking down the path, leaving Ingrid confused and unsure of what to do. While the figure was still in her sight, Ingrid finally made up her mind and followed the figure.

As they both walked down the path, Ingrid observed her surroundings, trying to figure out what was going on, and trying to figure out where this figure was leading her.

Suddenly the figured stopped, turned slightly, and waited for Ingrid to approach. When Ingrid was close enough, the figure pointed to the clearing where the mountains were covered by a thick blanket of snow, and where, beyond the mountains, lay the ocean of the North Sea.

"Am I supposed to...?" she began to ask the hooded figure, and then something about the figure seemed to be familiar. The figure still stood in the same stance, with its finger pointing, while a familiar sensation had continued to wash over Ingrid. She raised her hands over to the hood and drew it back. There was no face—just a white canvas of nothingness. Ingrid was not scared—just confused. She put the hood back, then looked at the path before her and proceeded towards the snow-covered mountains.

The journey to the mountains seemed to drag on and Ingrid was beginning to get impatient. Before she could say a word to herself out loud, a sound came from her left. Stopping in the middle of the path, she listened carefully to the sound. Suddenly the fox from one of her other dreams appeared from the bushes and gazed at her. He trotted onto the path before her, and then motioned her to follow him. Without a second thought, Ingrid followed the fox. After all, he was a familiar. They continued down the path for some time, for it was about a two-hour walk to the mountains.

As they made it to the top, between the mountains, the fox looked back at her and whispered, "Goodbye." Ingrid blinked and the fox had disappeared from her sight. She looked for the fox, but to no avail. From where she stood, Ingrid could see the North Sea that was inviting her. Taking a deep breath, she began her descent to the shore, which seemed to be laced with soft snowflakes.

After what seemed like an hour, Ingrid finally reached the shore. She stood there, enjoying the calmness around her. Suddenly the ground shook and rumbling occurred. Looking back, she saw figures emerge from out of nowhere, charging at her. Looking around, she found no place to hide. The only place she could go to hide was the water. She ran and dove into the water and kept swimming. She came up for a moment, to breathe and to see the shoreline. From where she was in the water, she could see all the figures on the shoreline looking for her. She could also hear some of them talking.

"Where did she go?" one asked.

"We need her now!" another yelled.

Ingrid wanted to get out of this dream, wanted to wake up, but something was not letting her. And then she heard someone speak. "I want her, I want you all to bring her to me now! And I want her alive."

The figure that spoke, stepped forward, and Ingrid could see it was a woman wearing dark green and black. The figure turned to look out to the sea, and Ingrid was more scared than ever. It was her.

Brutally, Ingrid was pulled down into the ocean waters and tried to escape. The hands grasped tightly onto her ankles and did not let go. Everything became black. After a few moments, Ingrid resurfaced and found herself lying on a different shore, staring out toward the cold North Sea. She looked at the sea and saw nothing. But the fox had somehow managed to waltz by and stared at her, then vanished. From a distance, she heard the woman's voice: "Bring her to me, now!"

"Please wake up, please wake up" Ingrid pleaded, out loud.

Chapter 11

WITHIN MINUTES, Ingrid found herself on the floor of her living room with her blanket barely covering her. "Oh, I must've fallen in my sleep," she groaned as she got up off the floor. Picking up the blanket, she placed it on the couch, and then made her way to the bathroom.

As she washed her hands, she glanced at the mirror and was not surprised at all. Her eyes were red and puffy, from crying herself to sleep. Her cheeks were flushed, and it looked like she had not slept well. After her hands were clean, she splashed some water on her face to help revive it. Drying off her hands and turning off the light, Ingrid headed to the study room and grabbed her journal and pen. She took it with her to the living room and sat on the couch. Staring at the journal, she knew what she wanted to say, what she felt. It was just a matter of making the pen contact the paper. She opened the journal to a blank page, and then began to write.

Pain, we all feel it. Some more than others, but nevertheless, we all feel it. And sometimes that pain will become a numbing sensation as all we want to do is shut off the pain, get rid of it. How do we do this? By killing it, by killing the pain. By killing the host that it resides in. That's how we kill it. I would know, I've always tried to kill it. I've tried so many times to kill if off with different methods, yet none have worked. And now, my dad has successfully killed it off. He killed it off by destroying the host, himself. And now, he is no longer here. And I miss him dearly. I miss him, yet am angry with him. Is it wrong for me to be angry at him? I just wish he had gotten some sort of help instead of letting it eat him alive. Soon, we must bury him, and soon I will get to say one last goodbye.

What is it that we are truly fighting? Is it each other? Or is it society? Correct answer: It is neither, for it is ourselves we are fighting. Constantly daily, we fight ourselves—the good and bad fight—while we stay in the neutral grey and try to not let the fight get out of hand. Can we ever stop this fighting? Who knows. Which side will win? Only time will tell. All I know is this: I'm afraid that the side of me that I hide could win. I do not wish for it to win.

Closing the journal, Ingrid placed it on the table in front of her and felt a tear fall from her eyes. Wiping it away, another appeared. Soon, a waterfall emerged, taking over her entire body. She grabbed the mug of now-cold tea and took it to the kitchen. She poured it down the sink, then her whole mind, whole body took over. She threw the cup into the sink, shattering it to pieces, and screamed. It was a much-needed scream that helped release a lot of the anger. She walked out of the kitchen to the front door and opened it. The cool air greeted her and she stepped onto the front porch (she hadn't taken her boots off), and she just stood there, letting the cool night air whip around her and try to take flight with her. And she would have gladly let the wind pick her up and take her away.

As she stood there, the stars in the sky shined brightly. There was no moon in view. Her eyes fixed on the constellations in the sky, while the icy breeze tried to make her shiver and send her back inside. But she didn't budge. Instead, she stayed on the porch and just soaked in the Icelandic night sky to calm her down.

She realized that she needed to call her boss and tell him what was going on, so she went inside and grabbed her mobile phone, then proceeded to call while she walked back outside.

A man's voice answered, "Hello?"

"Hello, Mr. Anton, It's Ingrid."

"Hello, Ingrid, what's going on?"

"Sir, you know I never ask for time off. But some personal matter has happened."

"What is it? You know you can tell me anything." He said with concern in his voice.

"My dad has passed away."

The phone went silent, and then Mr. Anton spoke.

"I am so sorry; you can have the next couple of weeks off. If you need anything, just let me know."

"Thank you, Sir. I will do so."

"Have a good night, and my prayers and condolences to you and your family."

"Thank you, Sir. That means a lot."

They both hung up, leaving Ingrid standing in silence on the front porch again.

As Ingrid stood on the porch, the cool Icelandic air whipped back and forth, trying to throw her around like a doll. But Ingrid didn't care; she let her body sway as she tried to keep her footing.

Letting out a sigh, Ingrid could feel it building up again. The tears were trying to force their way through every nook and cranny inside of her, hoping to win and make her cry even more. She felt it; she could feel the rise in her throat, the type of rise that made her throat ache with an unknown force. She tried to gulp in some fresh new air, to soothe the burning sensation that had taken place inside her throat, but that did not work. Instead, it had seemed to make it only worse.

While she continued to get frustrated with being unable to soothe her throat, Ingrid grabbed some snow off the banister of the porch and placed it in her mouth. She knew the snow was clean; no one had touched it. As the snow melted inside her mouth, slid down her throat, and calmed the burning sensation, Ingrid calmly took a breath, and just let herself be.

The silence that filled the nighttime air seemed to engulf the property, keeping it a hostage, while making sure no one would disturb it, as the energy around it reenergized. Ingrid did not mind being held captive by the silent night; in fact, she welcomed it with open arms. She knew that she needed the silence; she knew that the silence was where she would feel alive once more, and where she would be able to feel as though her father was still alive. This is what the silence had brought her. Unlike everyone else who needed the sounds of chatter to fill their minds to feel alive, Ingrid craved and needed the silence. It was her sanity, and not many people understood that about her.

Still standing on the porch, Ingrid's eyes scanned the night sky and played Connect the Dots with the stars. The cool north wind did not phase her one bit as it whipped around her red hair, creating a whiplash effect. It seemed to set a scene that Ingrid once imagined on the rooftop of her old childhood home. The scene was calm, and in her mind, it was what was keeping her from going insane and over the edge with what she had been dealing with. The news was still so new, and still overflowing from her mind. Ingrid felt that at any point she was going to capsize and lose herself to madness. She felt that she would spiral out of control, to the point where she would do something so drastic that she would not be able to come back from it. Just the thought of doing something so drastic sent shivers down her spine; she shook her head at such a horrid thought.

"Never," she muttered. "I will never do that."

Although she said she would never do anything that drastic, her mind was trying to convince her that there is no other way out of this grey area.

Suddenly, a beep from her phone emerged. The sound startled Ingrid, leaving her confused and curious about who could be texting her at that time of the night. She looked down at her phone to see who it was; it was a text message from Mathew.

"Hey! Just wanted to check in on you, and say hi. I will see you this weekend when I get back."

Ingrid did not want to reply at that moment, because she did not want to speak to anyone. She was angry, depressed, and felt like closing off the world to disappear for a few days.

"I'll text him tomorrow," she said to herself.

As she said those words, it seemed that a piece of iron had stuck itself into the words and her heart. This was very much unlike Ingrid, for it was never known for such a strong feeling to enter her, and leave her body in such a state of shock. The feeling lingered inside her core and left her more vulnerable to become numb.

Her face was now stoic, with her eyes all puffy and chapped lips from the continuous crying. Her body language gave off the defeatist vibe of giving up on everything, and just not giving a damn about anything.

Putting her mobile phone inside her jeans pocket, Ingrid turned around and walked inside, closing the door behind her. As she locked the door, she heard a rustling sound coming from the back yard, putting her on high alert. She walked through the hallway to the kitchen and peered out the window that overlooked the back yard. It was so inky-black outside that Ingrid could not see what might be out there, and she did not feel up to venturing out to the back yard where there was no light. Maybe it was just a wild animal roaming around outside. She did walk around her house after all.

After making sure everything was closed and locked, Ingrid made her way to the living room. She did not want to be in her own bedroom, and she certainly did not want to be anywhere near the guest bedroom. Being in the living room, she felt more in control of her mind. At the same time, however, she felt as though she was spinning out of control once again. The sensation of something dropping into the pit of her stomach overwhelmed her. She gulped hard. Her mind was spinning out of control. She felt like, even though she was sitting on the couch, she was going to fall so hard and so fast to the ground that she might not be able to catch herself. Ingrid decided to lie down on the couch. As soon as she did, her body jerked as if she had fallen from seven stories and crashed into the couch. This was very unusual or her, so she was uncertain of what just happened. She tried to sit up, and before she could, her mind began to spin out of control again, so she laid back down and just rode out the strange sensation.

"What the hell?" she said aloud.

Still lying down, she reached over to the remote and turned on the television to see a cooking show on. Not caring at all, she put the remote on the table and just watched the show as she rode everything out. Not what she wanted to go through; however, she had no say in the matter.

After thirty minutes, Ingrid decided to try again. Slowly, she sat on the edge of the couch, making sure she didn't feel the deep pit sensation again, and making sure she was not getting lightheaded again. After sitting on the edge of the couch for a few minutes, she realized that she seemed to be back to normal.

"Oh, thank God," she muttered.

Leaving the television on, Ingrid walked to the kitchen to pick up the mess she had created earlier. As she proceeded over to the sink, her eyes darted towards the window that was placed over the sink. Not being able to see outside, the thought of something or someone outside her window seeped into her mind.

"I'm being stupid," she said to herself. "There is no one out there. If anything, it's just an animal."

Picking up the broken mug pieces from the sink, Ingrid's mind careened in a different direction, making her feel that she was trapped in a trance, a trance that she would never escape. Her eyes were fixed on the broken pieces while her train of thought had figuratively wrecked...in another world. The sounds from the television did not take her out of the trance, just as the sound of the wind making the house creak didn't snap her out of it, either. Nothing would take her out, and it seemed that she did not want to be free of the trance. Seemingly, she was sorting through something in her mind, something that had been weighing her down.

Chapter 12

THE SCENE OF INGRID standing before the dark, cold North Sea played out in her mind, again. The wind stood still as the water sloshed back and forth ever so gently, the sand wedged between her toes, holding her in place. This place was so familiar to her, and she felt safe there, felt as though she could be at rest there. But where exactly was she? Breathing deeply, Ingrid realized that there was no fog surrounding her mouth, where her breath should be. She seemed to be in a place where no trace of wind could be found, which was impossible, and Ingrid knew that.

Still locked into the sand, Ingrid scanned the scene around her. The shadowy mountains seemed to make their appearance behind her, along with the lightless forest of dense trees. No other living being was near, leaving only Ingrid all alone on the shoreline next to the North Sea. Wiggling her toes in the sand, Ingrid realized that she was free from the soft pillows of sand that held her captive merely seconds ago. Shaking out the sand from between her toes, Ingrid continued to look around, and then a sudden sound made her jump.

The sound emerged from the tree line behind her. Even though she felt safe in the sand, she was still unsure about what lied in the trees. Part of her wanted to see what it could be, while at the same time, she was afraid to venture into the unknown forest. For some unknown reason, she found herself walking towards the tree line, while her mind was trying to persuade her body NOT to go there. Disquietingly, her body seemed to have a different mind controlling it.

Suddenly, she stopped just feet away from the forest, finding herself confused and wondering what was about to happen. As her eyes fixed on the trees, the sound of rustling continued not too far into the trees, making Ingrid even more nervous. As she stood there, rain began to fall, soaking Ingrid and the sand around her, creating a light muddy type of fixture to keep her locked into place once more.

"Hello?" Ingrid found herself saying out loud.

Why? Why would she speak to something that is not a familiar?

"I am stupid." She muttered to herself.

The rustling sound got closer to her, as if the person or animal wanted to show itself to her, but was afraid to come out of the forest.

"Hello?" a weak voice asked from the forest.

This stunned Ingrid; she did not know what to do or say.

"Who's there?" Ingrid asked the voice from the forest.

There was no reply; instead, silence filled the air once more.

"I will not hurt you. Please, who is there?" Ingrid asked again.

Again, there was neither rustling nor a voice.

As the rain continued to pour down, Ingrid was beginning to get impatient and concerned. She felt that she wanted to give up, since the voice seemed to have retreated into the ominous forest.

Soon, the rustling returned, making Ingrid hopeful that the person was okay.

"Hello?" Ingrid asked loudly. "Who is there?"

The rustling got louder and closer, making her feel both frightened and excited.

Soon a young man stepped out of the forest, standing in front of her with dark pants, a buttoned-down black shirt, and combat boots. His skin was tan; he had piercing green eyes and spiky black hair. For just a few minutes, Ingrid and the young man stood there in silence, staring at each other.

"Hello," Ingrid spoke.

The young man just continued to stare at her without saying a word, which made Ingrid feel uncomfortable. Then he spoke.

"Hello. You – you are Ingrid?" he asked with hesitation.

"How do you know my name?"

"Everyone here knows who you are."

This stunned Ingrid, and she began to scan the entire area to see who was watching them.

"Don't worry, no one else is around," the young man told her.

"What – ahem, how many people are there?" Ingrid asked, apprehensively.

"Over three hundred. Look, you shouldn't be here."

"Why?"

"I really can't say. All I can say is that you need to leave and never come back."

"No."

"Are you trying to get yourself killed?"

This jarring question startled Ingrid, she did not know if he was threatening her.

"I'm not leaving."

"Well, I can't make you…however, you should leave for your own good, especially if you don't want to get hurt."

Ingrid looked at the young man a little harder, and realized that she had seen him before, when she was wading back and forth in the water. He stood on the shore with all those other people and creatures.

"I know you…" Ingrid looked at him hard.

"I know I saw you staring at all of us from the water."

"Why didn't you say something?"

"I don't know."

"Well, why is there someone wanting me?"

"That I am not certain of, all I know is that I want to make sure you are safe."

"Thank you."

"Yes, well, you need to get out of here now, before anyone else finds you," the young man said as he scanned the entire area around them.

The young man went back into the forest, while Ingrid watched him walk away. She stood all alone on the beach once more, with the rain continuing to fall on her. She didn't care about the indifferent drizzle of rain. She was wondering how she was going to get out of this place, because it seemed impossible to get out of there, and it was starting to get to her. Looking around, she found three options: the sea, forest, or the mountains. Choosing one, she wouldn't know if it would lead her out or take her somewhere else that she wasn't prepared for.

Taking a chance, Ingrid made her way to the mountains. For some unknown reason, she felt drawn to it. It was an overwhelming sensation that pulsed throughout her entire body and mind, giving her a light queasy feeling in the pit of her stomach. As she stepped onto the trail that led into the mountains, Ingrid perked up her ears a little bit upon thinking that she heard something from the forest that begun to surround her, as the view of the ocean behind her began to disappear.

Ingrid didn't look back, for she wanted to put the memory of the ocean in the back of her mind. She continued along the trail and went deeper into the forest, becoming swallowed by the trees. The view of the sun had disappeared due to the thickness of the trees; however, there were little specks of sunlight that peered through the random parts of the branches and leaves, giving Ingrid some sense of relief, knowing that it was not yet dark and she would be safe for the moment. The trail beneath her feet was extremely soft, like the sand on the beach, and made her slightly slide as she walked up the trail.

As she continued to walk and slide a bit, she grabbed onto the branches that stuck out towards the trail, and caught herself a few times from falling face forward onto the trail. Out of nowhere, Ingrid heard a sound from the entrance to the mountain. It sounded as though a rock had been moved, and had rolled down the hill and crashed into something. This made Ingrid stand still, and made her more cautious about her breathing. Ingrid stood still, placed her hand on her mouth, and let her hearing senses heighten.

At the entrance of the mountain, a young woman dressed in a pine-green dress stood with four other people: one man, roughly six feet and five inches with brightly colored green-tipped blonde hair, stood next to the boulder that had been rolled from the entrance of the mountain. His muscular body did not seem to be strained by the heaviness of the boulder; in fact, he seemed very relaxed, and stared at the others. The other two men were the same height, with black hair and bright blue eyes. While one of them had freckles all over his face, the other had none. Their muscular builds made them seem intimidating. They were the twin brothers who were the body guards for their leader.

"Thank you, Johann," the woman spoke to the flaxen-haired man.

He grunted and nodded, not uttering a word.

"Now we must get in there and sort through all of this, and plan our next trap to get Ingrid," the woman said to those around her.

"Yes, and I have a feeling that she might be very near," another woman standing next to the twins spoke. She had short, spiked, bright pink hair, green eyes, dark caramel skin, and was about five feet and three inches. Slim in a sleek black jumpsuit with purple weapons strapped to her, she resembled an overgrown pixie.

"Near? Then we need to get things going now," the other woman spoke. "Everyone inside, now."

The four of them went inside the mountain, with Johann closing the boulder to the entrance. As the four of them hid behind the boulder deep in the mountain, Ingrid had walked up further on the trail, and was able to see all of them through the trees from where she stood.

"I have to get out of here," Ingrid said under her breath.

With that, she turned around on the trail and began to head back towards the ocean.

As she slid on the trail, she got closer to the ocean, and she began to hear noises rising from the trees. Bringing herself to a complete stop on the trail by holding onto a branch, the noise stopped as well.

"Hello?" Ingrid asked.

"What are you still doing here?" The voice asked from the trees.

"I'm leaving now. Why are you trying to push me out of here?"

"You are not safe. Get out, now."

"Get the hell away from me! I will leave of my own accord."

In an instant, the footsteps retreated, and Ingrid continued her way back to the ocean. As she reached the sandy shore of the beach, Ingrid had a strange sensation that someone was watching her. Although she tried to emanate the vibe of not being intimidated...deep down, she was terrified! As she stood in front of the cold ocean, Ingrid still had the feeling of someone watching her. She could not see a single soul lurking around, and she could not see those who might've been lurking in the trees, hidden by the thicket. Without a second thought, she began to run into the cold water, letting it swallow every inch of her, not caring whether or not she left.

"Damn it!" Ingrid snapped loudly. After nicking herself with one of the broken mug pieces, she was freed from the trance-like state. She put her finger in her mouth and tried to stop the bleeding.

She could feel the bleeding stop and pulled her finger out to see if it needed a Band-Aid. Realizing she did not need one, Ingrid picked up the last few broken pieces, in extreme irritation, and hurled them into the trashcan.

Exiting the kitchen, she took a deep breath and entered the living room, in an effort to calm herself. But as she walked in, her monstrous mind had betrayed her (yet again)…rampaging out of control; the room actually appeared to be moving, making her feel oh-so-dizzy and uneasy. Trying to grab onto something to steady herself, Ingrid blacked out and fell to the floor.

Chapter 13

MOMENTS LATER, Ingrid woke up, disoriented, finding her-self on the floor in the fetal position. Feeling so confused and slightly sore from falling to the floor, Ingrid slowly got up and made her way to the couch to comfort herself. Just the movement of her making her way closer to the couch exhausted her, made her wince from the pain. Having experienced this before, it was understandable for Ingrid to feel as though she had become foreign to her own house, to her own body, to her own mind, even as if this has happened before. *What is happening?* Ingrid wondered, in exasperation. Just thinking about what had occurred made her wince in pain, as if her mind had also been hurt from the abrupt fall.

Lying down on the couch, she lay her head upon the pillow, making sure she felt relaxed. Cradled by the couch and the pillow, she now felt safe and comfortable. For unknown reasons, her head felt more in pain against the pillow than if it were held up straight. Her body flinched from the pain. Ever so gently, Ingrid moved her right hand. Just the mere movement of this made her shudder, tear up. A small whimper escaped her mouth. With no one else living in the house, she would not be helped by anyone.

Unable to reach for her mobile phone, Ingrid just laid on the couch in fear of adding to the pain. For the longest time, she just laid there, staring up at the ceiling, wanting to find comfort in the moment. As she stared at the ceiling, a familiar sound alerted her. Her cell phone rang and she could hear how close it was. Slowly turning her head as she continued to flinch from the pain, Ingrid could see the phone lighting up on the coffee table next to her.

Panting and grunting at the same time, Ingrid moved through the pain, forcing herself to reach for the phone. Finally, Ingrid had the phone in her hand. Even though she was shaking uncontrollably and it seemed that the phone might slip, she had it. Without looking at the screen to see who it was, she hit the accept button, turned on the speaker, and spoke.

"H-hello?" Ingrid spoke as she panted heavily, trying to not burst out into tears.

"Ingrid?" A male voice spoke.

"Yes, who is this?"

"It's me, Eli."

"Oh, thank God."

"What's wrong?"

"I-I can't move. It hurts too much to move."

"What the hell happened?" Eli spoke rather loudly.

"I fell, and was barely able to make myself go to the couch."

"I will be right over."

"What? You are nowhere near my town."

"I am on the outskirts of the town, on the other side."

"Please, then, hurry."

"I'm on my way."

The line dropped, leaving Ingrid once again in agonizing pain on the couch.

Tears welled up in her eyes, the pain of her body shaking brought her even more tears. The deluge of tears streaming down her face seemed to bring her both comfort and pain. Then nothing. Ingrid saw only blackness.

Moments later, Ingrid heard in the darkness a familiar voice. "Ingrid!" The voice shouted, "Ingrid! Where are you?"

Although she could hear this person, and wanted to respond, it appeared that she had become mute and blind at the same time, as though her mind wished to introduce her to a world of darkness— darkness that she would never be able to escape.

"Ingrid?!" The voice approached the living room.

Even though she could hear him, she was still unable to speak or see.

"Ingrid! It's me, Eli." Her brother spoke quickly and loudly.

Ingrid moaned, to show him that she was still alive.

"I'm taking you to the hospital."

Without being able to verbally reject the notion, Ingrid went along with it. Ingrid felt her brother's hand cradle her head, then slowly nestle her neck and head, while his other arm nestled under the back of her knees.

"On the count of three, I'm going to pick you up. One, two, three...."

As soon as she was picked up off the couch, Ingrid let out a terrifying scream, a scream that communicated to her brother her pain and suffering.

"It's going to be okay, sis."

Eli made his way out the front door with Ingrid in his arms, trying to make sure that she would not bump her feet or head on anything. Gently placing her inside the truck, Eli got in on the driver's side and started it up, not waiting for it to warm up.

As they made their way down the road to the hospital, Ingrid's vision flickered in and out, but her voice remained nonexistent. "We're almost there; just hold on." Eli said, trying to reassure her.

Soon, they approached the front of the hospital doors. Eli turned off the truck, ran around outside to the passenger side door, flung it open, and raced inside the hospital, carrying Ingrid in his arms.

"Help!" Someone please help my sister." Eli yelled to a few nurses. One nurse ran in a direction to find a physician, another went to go find a room, and two nurses told Eli to carry her to the room as they all moved quickly down the corridor.

One of the nurses told Eli to put her inside a room, laying her on the bed. Once Eli placed Ingrid on the bed, the nurses moved him out of the way, while at the same time speaking to him as they hooked Ingrid up to the monitor and got her vitals.

Gathering all the information they could from the vital signs, and from what Eli could tell them, the nurses spoke with the physician before he came into the room. The 40-ish doctor walked into the room. He stood at eye level with Eli, with a few grey hairs woven into his brunette hair.

"Now, what is your name?" The doctor asked Eli.

"Eli, Sir. I'm her brother."

"Ah, yes. Now, I am Dr. Rolgburg, and I will be taking care of your sister. The nurses have told me how you have found your sister. From what I've gathered, it seems that she has slipped into a state of unconsciousness."

"What do you plan on doing to help her?"

"I will be running some tests, and will be keeping her for a few days. I must ask, are there any stress-related issues that have occurred lately?"

"Yes, we just lost our father to suicide; we are burying him on Saturday."

"Terribly sorry for your loss…If there is anything else you can think of that could have caused this, please let me know."

"Thank you, may I stay with her? I don't want to leave her alone."

"Yes, there is a chair over there. I'll have one of the nurses bring you a blanket."

"Thank you very much, Doctor."

"Very welcome," the doctor said as he left.

Eli settled into the chair that faced towards his sister, and just kept an eye on her, making sure to be there when she came to. The nurse came into the room, handed Eli a blanket and walked out. Draping himself with the blanket, Eli stared at his sister in the hospital bed, hooked up to the monitor, sleeping. As Eli sat in the chair and watched his sister, his eyes began to get heavy. He knew he was about to fall asleep, due to the fact that he had been driving all day, and that alone had made him tired. Trying hard to keep himself awake, Eli soon enough joined his sister in slumber.

Chapter 14

BUNDLED UP in a heavy coat, warm pants, and with her winter boots on, Ingrid walked through the chilly morning that surrounded her. She knew that she was dreaming, but she was unaware of how she ended up sleeping. Walking along the snow-covered road as the snow continued to swirl around her, Ingrid took in the brisk air, inhaled deeply, inviting the air to fill her soul and lungs, and then exhaled. As she continued to walk the path, her cheeks indulged in the harsh kisses produced by the wind, making them bright red. As she focused her sight on the road ahead, her mind began to wander off, past the road, past the snow-storm that was taking place before her.

The sound of the snow crunched beneath her feet, and every so often she would slip through the snow, catch herself, with each time shaking the snow from out of her boots. Making her way up the path, Ingrid looked around to find herself still alone in the forest, surrounded by huge trees that played shadows on the path ahead of her. She could see through the row of trees, and could see the mountains that called to her. Something about those mountains made her feel simultaneously comfortable and afraid.

Out of the blue, a sound emerged from her right side, from between the trees. Pausing, Ingrid's ears perked to figure out if they were human footsteps or an animal's. Then the sound ceased for a moment, as if it knew Ingrid was looking in its direction. Standing still on the path, Ingrid listened closer. As she looked between the trees, she felt her body start to reject her, reject her from the very spot she stood on, and wanted to eject her out of the area, to save her from whatever could be lurking in the forest.

The air around her stayed still and quiet, and the only sound Ingrid could hear was her own breathing. The sound of footsteps approaching, startled her like a deer-in-headlights. Not knowing what to do, Ingrid stood on the path, remaining quiet, hoping that whomever or whatever was in the forest would not see her or come out.

After a few moments, Ingrid heard the footsteps retreating into the forest, leaving her once again alone on the path. Letting out a sigh, Ingrid began to make her way up on the path, towards the mountain. As she walked up the path, Ingrid realized that this time, the weather was animated and she could feel every part of it. Knowing that this had never happened to her before, Ingrid began to wonder why it decided to happen. Her whole life, she never felt the wind brush against her face; she never felt the harsh kisses winter would normally produce, and to feel these things for the first time in her dream state made her feel slightly uncomfortable. She didn't adapt to sudden change in real life, and even in her dream state, she did not welcome the change, either.

As she ignored the cold wind pelting her now-ruddy cheeks, Ingrid kept walking the path, and it seemed to be never-ending, making her feel tired and agitated. At that point, she decided that she would turn around and just head back to the beginning of the path. As she turned around, she noticed that the trail was still there, but could also see that it led nowhere. Confused as to where the trail had gone, it now looked as though Ingrid did not have a choice but to stay on the snow-covered path, Ingrid kept her eyes on what was ahead of her, and her ears open so that she could make sure that no one would find her. With each step, Ingrid felt as though someone was watching her, but each time she looked around, she found no one. Shaking her head, Ingrid soon found herself just mere feet away from the top of the path of the mountain. This had given her a great view point of the land around her. She could see the tops of the trees, see the path that had led to somewhere unknown now, and could see the beckoning grey saltwater of the ocean on the other side of the mountain. Sighing with relief, Ingrid began to make her descent towards the ocean to see what was awaiting her.

As she got closer to the ocean, Ingrid began to wonder once again if there was someone watching her, since she had thought she had seen a figure lurking between the thick trees. Although she thought that she had seen something, she shook her head of such thoughts and just continued her way to the ocean. Just like the mountains, the ocean seemed to call to her, enticing her to venture towards its salty waters, begging her to take a dip.

Once again, Ingrid heard something from the forest, the same sound that she heard before—footsteps. These footsteps tried to be quiet, yet the sound of the snow crunching beneath their feet gave them away, giving away their position and alerting Ingrid of what might be hiding from her. Her ears perked up so much that they began to strain the muscles around them. It was with her ears perked that Ingrid could hear something once more in the forest. Knowing that there was certainly something in the forest, Ingrid didn't wait to find out who or what it could be, and took off running down the path towards the ocean. As she ran, she could hear someone running behind her, over her right shoulder. This made her run even faster, making her almost out of breath. She wanted to scream, but she knew that no one was around to help her, giving her no hope but to just keep running from whoever this could be.

As she reached the edge of the path, she heard the footsteps behind her running away, deeper into the forest, as if they did not want Ingrid to see them at that moment. Panting, with her hands on her thighs, and head down, Ingrid began to gain composure. The feeling of relief rushed through her entire body, letting her shoulders drop from the tense situation she had just dealt with. After catching her breath, Ingrid stood up and stared out into the ocean that was before her. She felt a wave of numbness wash over her, giving her an unsure feeling as to what just had occurred.

Stepping closer to the ocean, Ingrid took off her jacket, feeling as though she was overheating. As the jacket fell onto the sand, snow began to fall once more, creating a whimsical, ethereal world. Before Ingrid could even take one more step, darkness descended upon the entire scene around her.

Chapter 15

INGRID'S EYES FLASHED OPEN, welcoming the light of the hospital room, and the light that fell through the window from dawn descending upon them. Trying to move an inch, Ingrid felt a sharp sensation go through her entire body, stabilizing her and trying to force her to stay in the position. Turning her head, she could see Eli passed out in the chair with the blanket falling from his lap, his unkempt red hair sticking out even more, and his mouth slightly drooling. Ingrid smirked upon seeing her younger brother sitting next to her and sleeping. This showed how close she and Eli were, and showed how she had always been with her family. Making a sudden move made Ingrid moan very loudly, startling Eli from his slumber.

"Ingrid?" Eli moaned.

"Eli, I am hurting all over."

"It's okay, Sis. I'm here," Eli said as he moved the chair closer to the bed.

"What happened?" Ingrid asked, as she winced through the pain.

"I found you on the couch, out cold, and drove you to the hospital. You were not responding—well, vitals-wise you were doing well, but you were not speaking or seeing."

"Do they know what caused it?"

"No, but they've been checking your vitals and running some tests."

Directly, a nurse came into the room, surprised to see Ingrid awake. The nurse went over to the bed and began documenting Ingrid's vitals as she asked a couple of questions to Eli.

"When did she wake up?"

"She woke up just a few moments ago."

"Did she seem cognizant?"

"Yes, but she was pallid in color."

Then the nurse turned to ask Ingrid questions, watching her body reactions to how she answered the questions, while also seeing if there were telltale signs of issues that might be residing inside her body rather than outside.

"How are you feeling, Miss Ingrid?" The nurse asked.

"Alright," Ingrid spoke softly." I hurt very much; it hurts to move even an inch."

"Where does it hurt?" The nurse began to examine her body after removing the blanket.

"Everywhere, from my head all the way down to my toes. I don't know why, but I hurt. Make it stop." Ingrid pleaded.

"I will do what I can. Give me a few minutes, I am going to go talk to a physician."

With that, the nurse left Ingrid and Eli alone in the room, as they were once before. For a moment there was nothing but silence between them, with Ingrid's eyes staring straight up at the ceiling and with Eli staring at Ingrid, thinking about how all this could occur in the less than a week's time. First, their father committed suicide, and now Ingrid in the hospital. Eli worried for his family, for their health, their safety. He feared that everyone would be soon driven mad, down the deep rabbit hole…never to return.

Taking her eyes off the ceiling, Ingrid brought her eyes to meet Eli's eyes. Ingrid could see the worry, the fear, the fact that he was trying to hold back tears.

"Are you okay, sis?" Eli asked, making sure that his voice didn't crack, and give him away.

"I'm fine—ahem—I'm fine."

Even in the silence, Eli could tell that she was not fine, that there was something lingering in the back of her mind, but he couldn't figure out what it could be. But Eli knew his sister, he knew that he should not pry, that he should let her figure it out. And if she wanted and felt to, she would talk to him. Ingrid could always talk to Eli about everything, but there was something deep inside her mind that she refused to tell her own brother, for she feared he would not understand, she feared that he would think that she was crazy. That's what she feared the most. So, she kept her rambling thoughts inside her mind, locked away from her brother, her mother, from the rest of the world. She told herself that no one would ever find out, and that would keep her safe from the world's watchful and judgmental eyes.

Turning her attention from her brother to the ceiling, Ingrid soon heard footsteps entering the room. Slowly, she turned her head towards the door to see the physician standing at the end of her bed.

"Hello, Ingrid. My name is Dr. Rolgburg, your physician. How are you feeling?"

Barely able to move, Ingrid winced from the pain.

"If I stay still, I'm fine. If I move an inch, I feel as though I'm being stabbed multiple times."

"Sounds like you've had a nasty fall. Do you remember anything?"

"I remember…" Ingrid began, then stopped from the slight jerk of her leg. "I remember everything spinning, going dark, then after that, I fell. A little while later, I slowly made my way to the couch, heard my phone go off, briefly talked to Eli, then all went black and away…" Ingrid was about to speak of what she saw while she was out, but she knew that if she talked about such a thing, the doctor might send her to speak with someone about it, so she kept her mouth shut and fell silent.

Dr. Rolgburg watched Ingrid, wondering as to what she might say next, or do. He was curious, just as much as Eli was, about what was going on with Ingrid, so he was determined to help her.

"I would like to keep you here for a couple of days to run some tests." Dr. Rolgburg told her.

"No" Ingrid stated flatly.

"Ingrid, we must see what caused this."

"No, we are burying our father in two days; I cannot miss being there."

Dr. Rolgburg and Eli locked eyes, and Dr. Rolgburg motioned him outside the room.

"We'll be right back, Sis." Eli said.

Ingrid watched them exit the room, leaving her to her thoughts that stampeded through; this terrified and soothed her at the same time. After a few minutes, Eli and Dr. Rolgburg came back into the room with Eli taking his place once again by Ingrid's side in the chair. Dr. Rolgburg stood by the end of the bed and spoke.

"Ingrid, I just want to keep you till tomorrow morning. Can you do that?"

Ingrid thought for a moment then spoke, "Just till tomorrow morning?"

Dr. Rolgburg nodded.

"Yes, only till tomorrow morning. And that is it."

"With that, I am going to have my staff begin the tests right away. We will obtain blood samples, a urine specimen, do some orthostatic blood pressure tests and a few others. Today will be a long and busy day, not just for us, but for you as well. If at any time you feel strange or just feel like you need a breather, let one of us know."

Ingrid agreed, and then went back to staring at the ceiling. Dr. Rolgburg left the room, and the room was once again silent.

Silence was just a brief encounter before two nurses came into the room. One began to document vitals, and the other had Eli move away from the side of the bed so she could draw blood from Ingrid's vein. Normally, she did not mind needles, but with the already-present pain, the needle hurt so much entering that Ingrid wanted to scream. But all that escaped her mouth was a small whimper, and a few tears rolled down her face, giving away how vulnerable she felt, giving away the amount of pain she was suffering from.

"Alright, I am going to take the needle out," the nurse said.

"Okay," Ingrid answered breathily.

The nurse took the needle out, and Ingrid whimpered even more.

"It's okay," Eli whispered to her.

The nurse bandaged up her arm, making sure that no bruises formed and to be sure that the bleeding had stopped.

Taking the tubes of blood, the nurse began to walk out the door, but then she stopped.

"Do you think you could stand up, and go to the bathroom? We need a urine sample."

"I will need some help getting out of bed."

Ingrid winced as she brought herself up slightly on her elbows.

With that, Eli stood up and picked her up out of bed. Ingrid looked at her younger brother, terrified as to what he might see.

"Eli…" Ingrid began to speak.

"It's okay, I'm here to help," Eli whispered.

Both nurses followed them into the bathroom, and Eli turned Ingrid over to the nurses and closed the door as he exited. A moment later, Eli could hear the nurses talking to Ingrid.

"Alright then, we got it. Now, let's help you get up."

Eli could hear them trying to help Ingrid, but she was having difficulty standing up. It felt as if she were standing on shards of glass, and they were jabbing themselves up the soles of her feet, enabling her from taking a step forward. Then suddenly through all the pain, Ingrid planted her feet on the cold tiles and stood up with the help of the nurses.

"There we go. Do you think you can walk?"

Without answering, Ingrid took one small step, then another. Soon, she walked out of the bathroom with the nurses gingerly guiding her by her forearms, and with Eli watching them heading over to the bed.

Once Ingrid got back into bed, one nurse left the room with the blood and urine samples and took them to the lab, while the other nurse stayed in the room, preparing Ingrid for the orthostatic test. "Alright Ingrid, we are going to do some orthostatic blood pressure tests. The first will be lying down, then I will have you sit on the edge of the bed, and the final one will be with you standing. After each one, I will be taking your vitals. Okay?"

"Yes, I understand."

Ingrid took a deep breath as the nurse hooked her back up to the vital monitor to begin the test. After she was hooked back up, the nurse told her that the test was about to start, and told her to relax and not to talk or move. Listening to the nurse, Ingrid just laid there as the monitor beeped, gathering her blood pressure, oxygen, and pulse rate. Once the nurse documented the first round, she then went onto doing both the sitting and standing parts of the test. When the orthostatic test was done, Ingrid settled into the bed while Eli sat in the chair next to the bed.

"What are the other tests that will be performed today?" Eli asked the nurse.

"I will have to go look at my computer and see all the tests that Dr. Rolgburg put in," the nurse replied, and then left the room, leaving Ingrid and Eli alone.

"I am so—" Ingrid began to speak, but Eli cut her off.

"Don't. Don't be sorry, Sis. You are my sister...this is what family is for. We are meant to be here for one another."

Soon Ingrid began to cry, thus making Eli cry too.

"I...I miss Dad." Ingrid said through her tears and grimaced through the pain.

"I miss him too. Cannot believe he's gone."

By this time, they were both crying so hard that they were both having a difficult time breathing. They were still crying when one of the nurses came back into the room with a man attired in a crisp suit.

Eli looked up to see the nurse and the man standing in the doorway, and began to dry his eyes. Ingrid was already calming down when she realized her brother was staring at someone. She followed Eli's gaze, and saw the nurse and the man standing there in the doorway.

"Hello." Ingrid broke the silence.

"Miss Ingrid, this is Dr. Warren. He is here for the next test." The nurse motioned towards the doctor that stood next to her.

"Where is Dr. Rolgburg?"

"Dr. Rolgburg is working on a few things. However, Dr. Warren is here and available, and is going to run the next test."

The nurse left the room, leaving the three of them alone.

"Hello, Ingrid. It is nice to meet you. As she said before, I am Dr. Warren. Now," Dr. Warren turned his attention to Eli, "who might you be?"

"I am her brother, Eli."

"Nice to meet you, Eli. May I ask you to leave the room?" Dr. Warren asked.

"Why do I need to leave?"

"This test is highly personal. And since she is over eighteen, she does not need anyone to be in here."

"Regardless, she's my sister, and I'm here to protect her."

"Eli, I'll be fine. Go get something to eat." Ingrid said as she looked at Eli.

"Are you sure?"

Ingrid grabbed Eli's hand and assured him that everything would be fine. With that, Eli stood up and kissed the top of her head, then left the room closing the door behind him.

Dr. Warren walked over to the chair that was just preoccupied by Eli. He stared at Ingrid for a moment before he began to speak.

"Ingrid, this test is more psychological. I will just ask you a few questions, and you are free to answer them if you wish to. Would you like to start?"

Ingrid nodded in agreement, which prompted the doctor to begin.

"What was the last thing you remembered?"

"Last thing I remembered was falling to the floor, and then blacking out. After a while, I remember moving over to the couch, and then felt as though I couldn't move. Every time I tried to move, it hurt. It hurt so badly that I wanted it all to end. I do remember my brother calling me, and I briefly spoke to him, telling him what was going on. Then everything went black once more."

"Do you think you had hit your head or body on anything that might've caused the pain you've been dealing with?"

"Just the floor, I don't have many objects in my house or in my living room."

"Okay. Tell me, has this happened before?"

"Yes, this has happened several times growing up."

"Do you know of anyone else who might have gone through this?"

"No, no one that I could think of. You could ask my brother, or my mother."

"Where is your mother?"

"She is to be here today."

"Does she know what happened?"

"She might, if Eli has talked to her, then she will certainly know. But she is coming here for another reason."

"What is the reason, if you do not mind me asking?"

Ingrid stopped looking at Dr. Warren, pulled herself up into a seated position in bed, and then began to twiddle her thumbs.

"My..." Ingrid sighed, "my dad recently died."

"I'm terribly sorry. How long ago?"

"Just this past week. It was suicide."

"That must be very hard, especially on you."

"It's hard for all of us. He is a good man...brilliant...a dentist, a loving husband and father."

Ingrid noticed that she spoke of him in the present tense and not the past tense. Not only had she realized this, Dr. Warren noticed it as well, but he didn't bring it up.

"What do you think made him do it?"

Ingrid looked down at her hands, took a deep breath, and spoke.

"The monsters, the monsters that resided in his mind, the ones that he fought as he battled depression.

"Depression, such a terrifying issue one must deal with."

"It is even more terrifying when you deal with it daily."

"You speak of this as if you live with it."

"I do."

"How long?"

"Ever since I was a child—such a terrible waste of time dealing with something that has taken away parts of my life."

"Is that so?"

"Very much so."

"Have you ever seen a psychologist?"

"Yes, for my depression, and my Bipolar Disorder."

"Hmmm…" Dr. Warren rubbed his forehead.

This made Ingrid feel uncomfortable, uncomfortable with how Dr. Warren was reacting to the conversation. But Ingrid wanted to give Dr. Warren a chance. The conversation between them lasted for an hour and a half. Once finished, Dr. Warren left the room to go speak with Dr. Rolgburg.

After Dr. Warren left, Eli came back into the room.

"How did it go?" He asked with a worried look on his face.

"It went well, for being in a room with a psychologist."

"A psychologist?" Why on earth would they need to have you be seen by a psychologist?"

"It's just standard," Ingrid sighed as she tried to steer away from having a conversation with her brother about the psychologist.

"What do you think? Do you think I'll get to leave earlier, and not have to stay until tomorrow?"

"I do not know. All I do know is that I want you to get better."

"I will. I promise. Have you talked to mum?"

"Yes, she will be here within an hour."

"Good, I cannot wait to see her."

Hours seemed to have passed when the nurse came into the room.

"Miss Ingrid, I have orders from the doctor. You are to be released tonight. Your blood and urine results tested normal, vitals are stable; you will be free to go. The doctor has prescribed some pain medication. I will get your prescription ready, release papers, and you will be free to leave."

The nurse left, leaving Ingrid with happy news, and yet confused as to what the psychologist thought of her and the problem she encountered.

While they waited for the release papers, Eli helped Ingrid out of her hospital gown and into her clothes. Once she was fully clothed, Eli gave Ingrid his jacket, insisting that she needed to stay warm. As they continued to wait, they heard a knock on the door.

"Hello?" Ingrid spoke as she readjusted on the bed.

The door opened, and in walked their mom. She was the same height as Ingrid, and she seemed to be terrified of entering the room.

"Mom?"

"Oh, my baby girl. Are you okay?" She asked as tears filled her eyes.

"I'm alright, Mum. They are releasing me soon."

Isobel sat on the bed with her daughter, holding her and cradling her as she did when she was a child.

"How are you doing, my dear son?"

"Well, Mum. I am well."

"That's good. Is everything going okay at school?"

"Yes, everything is going well. Just constantly busy with school work."

"I imagine. Now, tomorrow we must go settle some things with the funeral home and prepare things for Saturday."

In silence they agreed. No one dared to object, nor did anyone dare to say a word to their mother. Not only did they lose their father, but she lost a husband, a man she loved dearly for thirty years: a man she devoted her life to, created a life and a family with. It tore her apart on the inside. On the outside, her two children could not figure out what was going through her mind, through her heart, so they felt isolated, unsure of how they were going to help their own mother through such a difficult time.

The nurse came back into the room with her hands filled with different types of papers. She sifted through them, making sure that everything was there, and then she spoke to Ingrid, barely acknowledging Eli or her mom.

"Ingrid, here are your discharge papers. Also in there are your lab results and notes written by the nurses, Dr. Warren, and Dr. Rolgburg. If you have any questions, please do not hesitate to ask. The doctor would like to see how you progress, so when you feel better, please come back for a follow-up exam. Here is the paper for the pain medication prescription. You are to take one pill every six to eight hours, no more than three times a day. There is only enough for a few days; the pain should subside by then. Do you have any questions?"

"No...Thank you for all you have done."

"Most welcome."

The nurse left, leaving the three of them alone together once more. Isobel stood up and motioned them to leave. Eli helped Ingrid get out of bed, helped her walk out of the hospital and get into his truck. Isobel drove her own car back to Ingrid's house, with her children behind her on the road, with Eli driving.

The entire time they were heading home, both Eli and Ingrid were quiet. The only sounds that were heard were the engine and the sounds of their own breathing. The radio was turned off, which bothered neither of them. It seemed in the sea of silence they could communicate.

Reaching Ingrid's home, Eli finally spoke.

"We're here. I think it'll be best if we all get some sleep"

"I agree."

Both vehicles pulled up to the house, parked, and all three of them went inside. Eli told them that he would take the guest bedroom, and suggested that their mom sleep in Ingrid's room. No one objected. As they got ready to go to bed, Isobel and Ingrid did not speak; they just got into their pajamas, climbed into bed, and fell asleep.

Chapter 16

STANDING THERE, Ingrid watched the snow fall all around her, floating down, like fluffy pillows that could fly in the night sky. The scene soothed her, comforted her, reminded her that no matter the trials she faced, or what health problems she endured or would endure in the future, there was the beauty in the breakdown: The beauty that lay in the stillness of night, in the silence of the darkness, in the moments where she felt as though she were going mad.

As she just stood there, she felt the snow settle ever so lightly upon her hair and face, becoming even more real by the second. Though it felt real, smelled real and even tasted real, she knew that she was in another dream state. This saddened her, for she wished to feel like this in her waking state, where she was free to roam, to express her emotions, but it appeared as she would never be able to. This frustrated her to no end, but here she gave that fear inside her head a dose of poison, which was silence. She had continued to watch the snow fall around her and just let it blanket her as she just stood there, giving herself to the darkness that the snow hailed from.

Just for a moment, all of her anxiety and fears were pushed to the back of her mind. All the stress she had been harboring since her dad committed suicide didn't fade away, but just hid in the corner, waiting to lunge back at her, making her very vulnerable once more. But she was not ready to be vulnerable again, nor was she ready to face the truth that her dad was gone. She knew, however, that it would not be up to her in the end, and she, indeed, would always be vulnerable.

Suddenly, she found herself lying in the snow, with a new view of it falling. This gave her a moment to rest...to just let the snow cover her, leaving her invisible to the rest of her surroundings. Lying there, she could hear off in the distance the roaring waters of the ocean, and this delighted her, for the sound of the water soothed her, along with the view of the snow falling on top of her.

In her mind, she wished to stay like this forever, to stay in this place, to never leave. But, sadly, she knew it would end. All she had to do was wake up, and then the entire scene would fade away, but she kept forcing herself to stay put, hoping to never leave. As she slowly stood up, she began to listen to the ocean water crashing even more. She wanted to find where the ocean was, wanted to be near the water once more, so, in the darkness and with the floating snow being its only light source, Ingrid made her way towards the sound of the ocean. Stumbling in the snow, she seemed to be in that familiar trance-like state, as if the ocean was luring her towards its icy, watery grave.

The sound of the ocean was extremely clear now, and the snow continued to fall around, melting as soon as it made contact. The smell of the ocean and the snow swirled around, then crawled up Ingrid's nose, delighting her senses with the unique fragrance that the water and air had created. Not wanting to move, Ingrid just stood there, in front of the ocean, as she listened to the music produced by the waves and enjoyed nature's fragrance. In that moment, she felt calm, as though everything from her waking life could not seep through and destroy her. She felt as though, there, she could run away from the roller coaster of emotions that she endured daily. And this made her feel happy. All this time, this is what she craved…happiness and calmness, since her waking her life had become nothing but a world of darkness filled with loneliness, misunderstanding, and confusion. Bitterness filled part of her life—especially when it came to her romantic life, due to her fear of her health scaring potential partners, believing that no one could handle her highs and lows, never knowing what her personality would be like when she woke up. Just standing there with the ocean in front of her in the darkness, and with the snow falling, her fear, the bitterness, loneliness, had been replaced by happiness, calmness, and love. Ingrid enjoyed this feeling, she had always wanted this, and to have these emotions…she finally felt normal!

The dark sea kept trying to lure her, kept trying to seduce her with the tuneful melancholy. It whispered incoherent sentences into Ingrid's ear while her eyes were fixed on the sea, fixed on the idea of losing herself to the chaotic waves that flowed back and forth. Then she snapped out of the trance due to a sound coming from the sea that hadn't been there before. Straining her eyes, Ingrid could make out a small figure approaching the shore: it was swimming in the water, bobbing up and down, struggling to reach the shoreline, and then it began to walk on land.

As Ingrid watched, she noticed it was the same exact penguin she had seen with Mathew on the beach. The penguin waddled up to her, looked her straight in the eyes, and didn't move at all. This took her by surprise, she didn't know what to do or what to think (and let's be honest: if *you* were in the dream state and saw the exact person or animal in your dream, you would be confused and weirded out). That's how Ingrid felt: entirely confused and weirded out.

Suddenly the penguin spoke, "Ah, nice to see you again, Ingrid."

Stunned...she was so stunned that she just stood there, staring at the penguin in disbelief.

"How..." Ingrid began to speak.

"How am I able to speak?" the penguin asked. Ingrid nodded and continued to stare at the penguin.

"I am a part of you, a part of your heart, your mind, your inner self. Therefore, I am able to speak to you."

"What about that day on the beach?"

"I was talking to you but only through actions. It seemed as though your mind was somewhere else, and I was unable to break through."

"And that's why you were acting so strangely, looking at me when Mathew was looking out to the sea."

The penguin nodded, and for a moment there was silence. Silence permeated the air around them as the snow continued to fall. In the midst of the silence, a sound came from the trees, jouncing both of their heads in that direction to see what could've made the sound. The sound from the trees occurred again, assuring the two of them that there was certainly something in the forest watching them.

"Ingrid, we need to get out of here. You are in danger."

"Danger? From what?"

"You know what from," the penguin said as he looked at her with his soft big eyes.

Ingrid knew what he meant, she knew who he spoke of, because she had seen the person with her own eyes. And she knew that she didn't want to meet that person face to face.

The sound from the trees stopped, and they both could take a deep breath and relax their shoulders.

"I am going to leave. But you must leave, you must leave now, I beg of you."

Ingrid watched the penguin waddle back to the ocean water and saw him disappear, leaving her all alone once more in the falling snow.

"I'm not ready," Ingrid spoke and then turned in the opposite direction of the path that would've taken her back into the clearing. She walked toward the mountains that awaited her presence. Cautiously Ingrid approached the entrance of the path that led deep into the mountains. She looked at her surroundings carefully, making sure that she didn't hurt herself by stepping into a hole... also keeping an eye out for anyone who might be lurking in the dark parts of the area.

Every time she took a step, rustling from the darkness would emerge, startling her, taking her attention from the path and shifting it to whatever was creating the sound. Ingrid wanted to shout to whoever was making the noises. She wanted to tell them to stop, but she was smarter than that. She knew that if she tried speaking to whomever it was, she would be in grave danger, and she wanted to stay out of danger.

Taking a deep breath, Ingrid kept on walking up the path through the trees, finally reaching the base of the mountain. As she looked around and down the path, she finally realized the rustling sound had stopped and she couldn't see any figures in between the trees. But she couldn't shake the feeling that there was still someone watching her from the trees—someone she, of course, could not see. Shuddering, Ingrid tried to shake the thought of someone staring at her. However, no matter how hard she tried, that nagging feeling in the pit of her stomach jutted up many red flags: One of them telling her to run; another telling her to wake up, to disappear quickly.

Deep down, though, Ingrid didn't want to wake up—not just yet. Instead, she turned and continued up the path around the side of the mountain, putting signs of danger in the back of her mind. "Keep going, you need to keep going," Ingrid spoke to herself as she continued the long walk.

As she kept reassuring herself, the voice in the back of her mind kept warning her to turn back. Each time she kept fighting it, telling it to go to hell and leave her alone. Ingrid knew that she needed to listen to this instinct of hers; she knew it was trying to keep her safe but, with her natural stubbornness, she didn't want to cave in. This always got Ingrid into sticky situations that usually took a decent amount of time to get her out of, and she knew that, but at this moment in time, Ingrid didn't care. She wanted to know exactly who was awaiting her up on top of the mountain.

It seemed like hours—it always did—but this time, the walk up the side of the mountain felt as though she had wasted half a day just trying to make it to the top. Once she finally reached the top, she was greeted by a sense of warmth, the type of warmth that would only come from wood being burnt to keep campers warm, or those cozy in front of their home fireplaces. Looking around, Ingrid finally saw a small campfire. Shocked, she was even more worried when she saw a group of people sitting around the campfire—especially when she recognized one of the men! She had seen him once before, standing on the shoreline with the group of people searching for her near the ocean. Up close he looked even more like a giant, and his muscles were as big as Ingrid's head. This frightened her. At this point, she had no clue what to do and wanted more than anything to get out of there and run quickly.

Slowly taking a step back, a pebble started tumbling down. This startled the entire group around the campfire, making the giant stand up rather quickly.

"Stay here," his voice boomed.

All the others listened and stayed where they were. As the man looked around the top of the mountain, Ingrid cowered into a dark corner, hoping that he would not find her. Suddenly, the man stepped right in front of her. From Ingrid's point of view, she could see him in all his glory, and she hoped that the darkness concealed her. Although she hoped that so much, the man spotted her cowering, bracing onto the side of the corner, trying to shield her entire being with the darkness. There was something about her that he wanted to protect; he just couldn't quite figure it out.

"Anything out there?" one of the members of the group yelled out.

A brief pause made the air silent, too silent.

"No. Nothing is here," he replied, then turned to go back to the group.

With this opportunity, Ingrid slowly and quietly made her getaway down the path to the ocean. As she walked down the path, she could hear pebbles behind her slowly making their way down to her, greeting the pebbles she was dragging along. Stopping, Ingrid then realized that the pebbles behind her stopped, and so did the light footsteps that were once there. A sensation of wanting and not wanting to know who was behind her began to take over her entire being. She soon gave in.

Turning around, Ingrid was greeted by the giant man standing behind her. For that moment, there was nothing but silence—pure silence—no snow, no gravel moving, no wind, nothing.

"Let me take you to the shore," the giant spoke.

"Why should I trust you?" Ingrid asked, with hesitation.

"You don't have to trust me; you just need to know that I can make it safer for you to get to the shore."

Looking at the giant man, Ingrid couldn't shake the feeling that she somehow, someway, knew this man. There was something in his face, in his eyes, in his body language, that seemed rather familiar, but she couldn't place her finger on it. All she knew was that she could trust him to get her back to the shoreline, to get her back to safety. As they began walking down the path, Ingrid began to realize that she is walking right next to the mountain with the giant man closer to the edge of the path, sheltering her from the elements, and also protecting her.

Halfway down the path, they both were completely silent. It appeared that the giant man was on guard. The look on his face was determined, as though if anyone or anything were to come at either one of them, he would be fully—mentally and physically—prepared to take them on. Just as they were about to reach the shoreline, Ingrid looked at the man again and couldn't shake that feeling she still felt about him.

"Who are you?" Ingrid finally asked as they reached the shoreline, and as her eyes stayed fixed on the ocean waters. For a moment, there was nothing but silence, and then the man spoke.

"My name is Torryn," he said in his deep voice.

There was no need for words between them; it seemed that they could communicate without words, as though there was a link or bond between them. Ingrid was worried. She was not afraid of this man; however, she knew that she should be since she knew that he was part of the other side. But she felt comfortable, felt safe; he felt familiar. Ingrid just could not place why she felt like they had met before.

"I must go and so must you," Torryn spoke in a low voice as his eyes scanned the area.

Ingrid nodded her head in agreement and watched Torryn walk back up the pathway and out of her sight before returning her gaze towards the sea at her feet. Taking a deep breath, Ingrid came to the realization that she did have to wake up, that she did have to deal with everything, but she didn't Feel. Quite. Ready. ...Ingrid took another deep breath and slowly walked into the cold grey sea.

Chapter 17

THE SOUND OF someone moving about in her bedroom made her eyes flutter open, then Ingrid came to realize that it was her mother having been getting ready for the day. Ingrid slowly began to move in bed, stretching and moaning, making sure that none of her muscles were tense. Noticing her daughter doing this, Isobel went over to the Ingrid and gave her a kiss on the forehead.

"How are you, Love?" her mom asked with a concerned look upon her face.

No words came out of Ingrid's mouth—just more moans. Isobel became more concerned, but finally, Ingrid spoke.

"I'm alright, Mum."

Isobel's face softened, but the concern on her face was still noticeable, and Ingrid noticed it without a doubt.

"I promise, Mum. I'm alright," Ingrid said, trying to reassure her mom, but that didn't help a whole lot. Ingrid got out of bed, motioning her mom away so she could get ready. Not wanting to leave her daughter alone, Isobel stayed in the room, keeping an eye on Ingrid as she slowly walked around the room and got dressed. She watched her slowly rifle through her dresser, picking out clothes and going to the bathroom to take a shower.

"If you need my help, let me know," Isobel said as Ingrid closed the door.

Hearing the shower turn on, Isobel tightened up even more. Her fear of her daughter getting hurt in there worried her so much that she wanted to barge through the door and check on her. But every inch of her also rejected that notion simply by stating that her daughter was okay, that if Ingrid wanted her, she would simply call for her. So Isobel waited for Ingrid to emerge from the bathroom.

The sound of the shower water stopped and Isobel loosened up slightly. After a few minutes, Ingrid came out of the bathroom, fully clothed and drying off her long red hair with a towel. Isobel watched her daughter move slowly around the room as her eyes scanned for something important.

"Are you looking for something?"

No reply came from Ingrid's lips. Instead, she just kept looking around the room. She didn't want to tell her mom that she was looking for her journal—the journal that would tell her everything, the journal that would have every emotion and every dream slip out into the real world, the journal that would give anyone who would read it nightmares—so Ingrid kept her mouth shut and continued scanning the room. It was after searching the entire room that Ingrid realized where she had left the journal: in her study room on the side table. Ingrid knew that it would be safe in there, so she left it alone and turned her attention to her mom.

"Mum, do you want some tea or coffee?"

"Coffee sounds good, Sweetie," Isobel said as she continued to watch Ingrid walk around the room.

Opening the door, Ingrid left her mom in the bedroom and still concerned about her well-being. But she didn't want her mom to worry about her. She didn't want any pity, either, especially from her own mother. As Ingrid entered the kitchen, the sound of her mom's footsteps followed behind her.

"I'll go start the coffee, Mum. Go ahead and grab a cup from the cupboard."

As Ingrid made the coffee, the sensation of someone's eyes on her back burned into her flesh. She knew in that instant her mom was watching her once more, but this time with more intensity. She wanted to say something to her mom to make her stop worrying so much, but she knew that no matter what she said to her mom, she would not stop worrying. She knew her mom, and she knew that she worried constantly about her children. It was just part of her personality.

"Hand me your cup, Mum," Ingrid said without looking at her. She didn't want to look at her. She knew if she did, she would see the sadness and concern in her eyes. She, of course, could understand the sadness because her mom did lose her husband, just as she had lost her dad. Ingrid stretched out her hand towards her mom, took the cup and filled it with coffee.

"Thank you, Sweetie," Isobel said after taking a sip.

"Welcome, Mum," Ingrid said as she grabbed a cup and poured herself some coffee.

The sound of footsteps coming down the hallway filled the house as they drank their coffee in the kitchen in silence. Eli emerged from the hallway and appeared before them all dressed and holding his keys. He could feel the tension, and immediately became unsettled by it, so he decided to break the silence.

"Morning, Mum," Eli said after kissing her cheek.

"Morning, Dear," Isobel replied.

Eli grabbed a cup and poured himself some coffee and gave Ingrid a kiss on the cheek. "Morning, Sis."

Ingrid smiled. "Morning, Bud."

After they all finished their cups, they put them in the sink and began to head into the hallway near the front door. They each pulled on their boots, jackets, and made sure they had everything before heading outside.

As Isobel and Eli went to the truck and warmed it up, Ingrid locked the front door, then ran over to the truck and climbed in on the passenger side with her mom sitting between her and Eli. Slowly they backed out of the driveway and made their way over to the funeral parlor to discuss the burial decisions. All three of them were uncomfortable, because no one wanted to discuss how to bury someone they loved so dearly. As they made their way down the road, they were cloaked by silence. The only sounds that could be heard were the heater filling the cabin of the truck and the engine that was working a bit harder due to the harsh winter that seemed to make their journey that much harder.

As they approached the funeral parlor, the tension between all three of them increased. This made Isobel more aware of her children's body language. She saw the look on Eli's face became more stoic, and his entire body tensed up, locking into place. As Isobel turned to look at Ingrid she could see the big difference between her son and daughter in this devastating situation that they were thrown into. Ingrid's entire body resembled a Raggedy Ann doll, just limp and merely placed there. Her hair seemed to be invested in shielding her face from her brother and mom, making sure that neither one of them could see the look on her face. As her hair concealed her face, it concealed the most important thing from her mom: Her eyes. If Isobel were to consider Ingrid's eyes, she would see that they were nearly empty. No, they were not dark or contemplating something bad. Her eyes just portrayed what was happening inside her. Deep inside, down in the pit of her soul, she felt empty. She felt that way when she first found out about her dad's death.

As they continued to drive down the road, Isobel every now and then looked at both of her children as their attentions were on different things. Eli's full attention was on the road ahead of them, while Ingrid's attention was somewhere off in the distance. The silence didn't bother Isobel; in fact, she didn't mind it at all, but what she did mind were her two children, whom she was worried about. She wanted to reassure them, to tell them that everything would be alright, but she didn't know exactly what to tell them. She was not skilled with this sort of situation. She had lost her parents a few years ago when they were in their old age and had already lived long lives. Both of them had passed away in their sleep at the ages of eighty-eight and eighty-two, just months apart from each other. Everyone was prepared because they knew that they were up in age and it was their time to move on. But with her husband, he was still young. He still had a long career ahead of him, and he had such a short life. He still had so much to do, so much to see, so this was indeed not his time to die yet. Isobel was extremely uncomfortable with how to comfort her children. She couldn't just hug them and tell them that life will go on and the best thing to do is to remember their father in a good light. If she did that, what would they do, what would they say? Isobel simply stayed quiet the entire ride.

They pulled up to the funeral parlor and climbed out of the truck. As they walked inside the small building, they were greeted by a woman who seemed to be of middle age. Her black hair was pulled back and her pale skin stood out against her swarthy features and vibrant red dress.

"Hello, how may I help you?" the woman asked as she looked at all of them with a slight smile.

"Hello. We are here because of the death of my husband, their dad." Isobel said softly.

The look on the woman's face sunk, because she then realized who they were. She had received his body just the other day and expected the family to arrive within the next few days.

"You are Arthur Anderssen's family?" the woman asked.

They all nodded in agreement.

"Follow me. You will be speaking with my husband for the burial arrangements." The woman guided them through the parlor to the office where a man sat behind the desk with his eyes on the screen before him. The woman knocked on the door and cleared her throat to let him know there was a family to see him.

The man turned his head and saw his wife with the family

behind her, and stood up.

"Thank you, Dear. Please, come in." the man said as he directed them to the chairs in front of his desk. "How can I help you to-day?" He asked as they sat back down.

This time Eli spoke. "We are Arthur Anderssen's family. I am his son, Eli; this is my sister, Ingrid; and this is our mom, Isobel."

"Ah, I am terribly sorry for your loss. Suicide is a horrible way to lose someone."

The threesome's silence was in agreement with his remark.

"My name is Jon Grimsson and I'll be helping you with all of the arrangements for the burial."

With this, the conversation of burying Arthur began. Ingrid was still empty and didn't seem to really know what was happening around her, but she tried to listen to the entire conversation that happened between her mom, Mr. Grimsson and Eli. They discussed the traditional burial rituals, and a few modern burial options. They all talked about the different ways that would not break the bank yet would also go along with what Arthur had stated in his will that he had drawn up and signed a few years ago. After what seemed to be an hour of discussion, they all agreed on proceeding with cremation and placing the urn inside a grave. Ingrid came to, and even agreed with this final decision. Then, out of nowhere, Ingrid's mind transported her back to her dream world, even though she was very much awake.

Chapter 18

INSTEAD OF emerging from the ocean or near a clearing, Ingrid found herself deep inside the forest. Looking around, she could not figure out what was going on, nor could she figure out where she was. She had never been there before, and she didn't know how she got there. She knew for a fact that she was very much awake and was with her mom, brother, and Mr. Grimsson, picking out urns for the ashes of her dad; so the sudden start from the coldness of the dream world made her feel rather confused.

While she continued to scan the area for an escape, a sound made Ingrid more aware of her surroundings. Heavy footsteps were moving in her direction, and by how much noise they made, she could tell that whoever it was, was struggling to be quiet, trying not to scare her off. The only thing Ingrid could think of doing was hiding underneath one of the overgrown parts of a small hill. She knew that if she ran, she had a higher possibility of running into whomever it was. Slowly, she made her way over to the small indent under the overgrown hill, and wrapped her arms around her legs, bringing them closer to her chin. Keeping her mind focused, she began to focus on her breathing. She didn't want to hyperventilate and bring whomever it was in her direction.

The footsteps got closer, and Ingrid could also hear a deep voice muttering. She couldn't figure out who it was, nor could she figure out what was being said, but she was terrified! The footsteps stopped right above her head. Ingrid tried to keep her breathing silent and tried not to cry, then suddenly, she heard a voice softly speak out.

"Miss? Are you here?" the deep voice asked softly.

Silence—the voice that had just spoken was greeted by silence. He knew that Ingrid was around, but he didn't want to terrify her. He moved slowly onto the small path that was right below him. The entire time, Ingrid began to get even more nervous as he got closer to her. Finally, she could see the boots right in front of her.

"Miss, can you hear me?" the voice spoke once more.

This time the voice sounded quite familiar to Ingrid: *Torryn.*

"Torryn?" Ingrid asked.

The feet turned to the right.

"Miss?" The voice asked again.

Ingrid slowly came out of the hole and greeted Torryn. She never thought she would be so glad to see him, but she was, because she felt safe with him, and it seemed that deep down they knew each other in some way, shape or form.

"Miss, what are you doing here?" Torryn asked with a concerned look on his face.

"I don't know. I was with my family and Mr. Grimsson, and I was brought here."

"Who is Mr. Grimsson?"

"He is a funeral director."

"Who died?"

"My dad." That was all that Ingrid had to say and Torryn felt sorry for her.

"Sorry," he softly spoke.

"Thank you."

"I need to get you out of here."

"Where am I exactly?"

"You are deep in the forest of Branmoor. You are not supposed to be here."

"I honestly don't want to be here. And quite honestly, I don't even know how I got here," Ingrid admitted, feeling drained.

Tension bristled between them, but a sound from the forest instantly put them on high alert. With no warning, Ingrid began to feel dizzy, and Torryn's face came blurry as she fell to the ground. The last thing she could remember hearing before blacking out completely was the sound of Torryn's concerned voice trying to wake her up as he lightly shook her.

While Ingrid was out cold on the forest floor, Torryn was on his knees trying to figure out what exactly had happened, then he found the dart that protruded from Ingrid's back.

"What?" Torryn said out loud.

"So, you thought you could keep her from me."

An aggravated voice came behind him. Torryn's face became stoic yet highly concerned as soon as he heard the voice.

"I don't know what you mean, Madam," he replied, trying to assure the person that he wasn't trying to keep Ingrid from them.

Slowly, Torryn rose and turned towards the direction of the voice. Right before him was a woman who could be Ingrid's identical twin sister. The only difference between the two of them was that this woman wore completely black clothing, and the tips of her red hair were purple. The only real problem was the fact that this was Ingrid—her other half, the other part of her mind, the part of her mind where the ever-swirling turbulence of her depression and intensity existed.

"Well, Torryn?" She asked with one eyebrow raised.

Torryn still did not say anything. He knew that it would only make things worse, so he stood in complete silence, standing in front of Ingrid's body that lay motionless on the forest floor.

"You knew I was looking for her, and you hid her from me. That is an offense. I am taking her and you will be tortured for betraying me."

Torryn did not disobey or try to argue with her, for he knew what would happen if he did.

A man emerged from the forest, picked up Ingrid's body, and slung her over his right shoulder as if she were nothing but a sack of potatoes. He then followed the other Ingrid up through the forest and onto the dirt trail that awaited them. As they all walked in silence with Torryn up at the front with his wrists bound by chains, none of them were aware of someone tracking their every move and following them through the thickest parts of the forest. It was as though the footsteps this stranger was making were completely silent, as if by some sort of magic, as if they had given themselves the ability to become completely quiet so that no one in the world would ever be able to hear them.

As they continued up the path, Ingrid's eyes began to open

slowly, trying to adjust to the scene that was playing out for her. Realizing that she was slung over someone's shoulder, Ingrid tried to figure out what she could do to get out of the situation. She knew that if she started to kick and scream, something would happen to her. All she could do was pretend that she was still asleep so nothing bad would happen. The entire time she looked around the area to try and find a way to escape, she saw something moving in between the trees. Although all she could see was a silhouette moving about, she could tell that there was another one right behind that silhouette that seemed to be looking in her direction.

After a while, Ingrid could hear other voices having conversations as they approached the mountain. Hearing these voices, Ingrid closed her eyes and pretended that she was still out cold, making sure that her body was not tensed up as they approached the others. Voices buzzed about, but as soon as they came into view, they stopped. She was unable to open her eyes, for she was afraid that there was someone or something looking at her. Her ears perked up and could hear someone's breath right next to her face, as if they were examining her. Although every inch of her was fighting the urge to open her eyes, she wanted so much to just get one glance at the being that was staring at her, breathing on her, and the feeling inside her chest made it harder for her to keep on pretending that she was asleep.

Suddenly, Ingrid felt herself being laid down on some sort of fabric, then felt a hand on her back grasping at the dart and pulling it out. She flinched a little from the pain and from the roughness the dart was pulled out with.

"What the hell…" a woman's voice said.

"What?" a man's voice asked.

"Don't hurt her. She is to be kept safe, not hurt," the female voice spoke.

"Sorry, Boss. Didn't mean to."

"You are truly remarkable, you insufferable idiot." The female voice stated. "Now, go. I want to be left alone with her."

The man retreated outside, away from the ladies, leaving Ingrid alone with this unseen person. All she knew was that the voice seemed familiar, too familiar. To her ears, it seemed that it was her own voice that had just spoken.

"I know that you are awake--I'm not stupid like the others" the voice spoke.

A lump formed in her throat, and every inch of her body wanted to retreat inwards, to get out of there, away from whomever it was. She could hear the person walking around, and at moments she could tell the person paced back and forth in front of her body. As Ingrid listened to the footsteps, she had not picked up on one sound…then suddenly…*splash!*

Ingrid bolted upright, water having been poured on her face and hair.

"Well, hello. We finally meet face to face," the voice said from behind her.

As Ingrid tried to dry off some of the water, her face turned red. Realizing that the voice came from behind her, she stood up so fast that her feet kicked the fabric that was laid beneath her body as she turned towards the direction of the voice. Right before her eyes, Ingrid was looking at herself. At first, she thought it was a mirror, or an illusion. Then she realized the differences between them. Ingrid had realized that her eyes were wider than usual while staring at herself.

"Hello," the woman hissed, with a smirk.

Ingrid did not say anything. She didn't know what to say. And she certainly did not want to be near this woman, even if she was, in theory, herself.

"Well, since you are not going to say anything, I might just tell you where you are."

Ingrid continued to look at her with a blank expression, unsure of what to make of this person.

"You are in my land. This camp is nestled deep in the base of this mountain where no one else is allowed, and all of those who dare enter are considered trespassers. We share the same name; however, everyone calls me either Inga or Boss. Do you know why I wanted you here?" Inga asked Ingrid.

"No," Ingrid finally spoke.

"I want you to join us fully. Just imagine if the both of us were on the same side instead of fighting each other for the next fifty to seventy years. It would—"

"No," Ingrid spoke.

"Now, look—" Inga said quickly.

"No, I said no. I am not joining you."

"But wouldn't you rather see your dad one more time?" Inga asked with an arched eyebrow.

This caught Ingrid off guard and unsure of what was going on.

Inga chuckled. "Oh, yes. He might be dead in your world, but he is very much alive here, for now."

"That's impossible!" Ingrid's voice cracked.

"Nothing is impossible," Inga smirked again.

"Let's go say hi to Dad, shall we?" Inga continued. She turned her back to Ingrid and walked out of the massive tent, not waiting for her to follow. Inga knew that Ingrid would follow behind, and she was right. Ingrid walked out of the tent and saw Inga walking towards a caged area where a man was chained up. With that queue, Ingrid walked over to the chained-up man and realized who it was. It was Torryn.

"Torryn?" Ingrid asked with a confused look.

Torryn looked at Ingrid with his teary eyes, not saying a word. He then turned his head away, and slowly tugged on the chains that seemed to be controlled by magic.

"What?" Ingrid asked.

"You didn't know? This is Dad." Inga said.

"No, he's not!" Ingrid said bluntly.

"Actually, yes, he is." Inga replied. "Does he seem familiar to you? How about the way he looks at you? How about the way he talks?" Ingrid thought about it, and to herself she said yes to all the questions. He did seem familiar, and she never knew why. After much thought, and putting the pieces together, she realized that Torryn was indeed her dad, just in another form. The same way Inga was the other world version of her, Torryn was this to her dad. And in that moment, she wanted to save him, to finally free him.

Inga walked away, leaving Ingrid with Torryn, fully unaware of what was to come. While Ingrid considered the cage where Torryn was being held, sadness and rage began to build up: Sadness because she had been missing her dad, and rage for the fact that he had left her, and all of it was boiling inside of her, wanting to be released. Ingrid looked more at Torryn and noticed tears streaming down his face, but no noise came out of his mouth. It was the look of defeat and sadness on his face that made her even angrier.

Ingrid felt her hands grow hotter as her rage climbed higher, and then she felt like she was on fire. Looking down at her hands, Ingrid saw fireballs. For a moment, she questioned why this was happening. She looked around before turning her attention back to Torryn. Seeing him in the cage fueled the anger and made the fire grow stronger in her hands. Looking around one more time to make sure no one was watching, Ingrid readied herself, then started throwing the fire at the cage's padlock. After a few times, the padlock finally dissolved and the door opened slowly. Opening the cage door, a little more, Ingrid stepped inside and stood in front of Torryn, who was still looking at the chains around his wrists.

"I'm getting you out of here," Ingrid said stoically.

Torryn didn't say a word. He just sat there in silence, still staring at the chains. Then he finally spoke, "I'm sorry that I let you down."

Taken aback, Ingrid stood there in shock for a moment. She then realized that they had very little time before anyone would come over.

Focusing on the fire in her hands, she intensified her anger and the fire roared, with bits of flame sparking off onto the ground. She threw a few fireballs at the chains, with each one damaging them more until ultimately they fell off. Ingrid grabbed Torryn's hand, letting him know that it was alright, and letting him know that he didn't let her down.

"Let's get out of here," Ingrid whispered.

"We need to go this way," Torryn said as he pointed towards the direction of the trees.

The two of them slowly moved over the trees while they scanned the area, making sure no one saw them. As they entered the forest, the voices of those back at the camp got louder. They seemed to be worried and terrified. Then, suddenly:

"You let them get away! Go find them!"

They both realized the voice came from Inga.

Running through the forest, Ingrid and Torryn never once looked back. Their focus was fully on the path that was before them. They jumped over fallen trees, slid down hills, and even at one point encountered a bear that just stared at them. All of this seemed to be the only thing that their minds focused on—well, that and the thought of getting far away from Inga and the others. Little did they know that Inga was not far behind. She could see their every move as she ran through the trees. Suddenly, Ingrid and Torryn found themselves at the edge of a cliff with the roaring grey ocean below.

"Where do we go now?" Ingrid asked, catching her breath.

"Uh—" Torryn replied. His eyes scanned the area. He realized the only two ways to leave were either jumping off the cliff, or turning back into the forest. A sudden sound from the forest stopped his thought, and he realized that the forest was no longer an option.

"Stay next to me," he whispered.

"What?" Ingrid asked. Then she heard the sound that came from the forest.

Moving closer to Torryn, the sound got closer until the person who created them emerged. Inga walked out of the forest with a smirk on her face.

"Well, well, look what we have here."

Torryn and Ingrid tried to back up a little bit, but they knew if they moved anymore they would be in the ocean, rolling around in the waves.

"Leave us alone!" Ingrid shouted.

Inga moved closer, eyeing Torryn. "You know you are supposed to be on my side."

The tension between them grew, and Torryn's face flared red with anger and resentment.

"I'm no longer on your side." He wrapped his arm around Ingrid.

"Too bad," Inga said, raising her hands to reveal fireballs, and aimed one at Torryn. Before she could throw one, Inga was knocked to the ground by a fireball: One that came from Ingrid. Ingrid raised her hands again to throw another one, but Torryn stopped her.

"You need to go," Torryn stated.

"I'm not letting you go again," she said as a tear rolled down her cheek.

"I'll be alright, I promise."

"How touching," Inga said as she rose up.

"Go, now!" Torryn said as he pointed towards the sea.

Ingrid gave him one kiss on his cheek, and Torryn started charging towards her. With the two of them fighting, Ingrid contemplated jumping, but at the same time she wanted to save Torryn. She looked out at the sea, then at Inga and Torryn fighting. She knew that before she could leave, she had to do something. Concentrating on everything that held her back, on every ache and pain, on losing her dad and herself, she could feel the intense fireball form in her hands. Looking at Inga, the fireball grew more intense, and in that moment, she knew what to do.

Taking aim, Ingrid waited for the right moment, then yelled.

"Hey, Inga!"

Both stopped for a moment to see the giant fireball.

"It's time for YOU to go!," she shouted. Then she threw a fireball at Inga, incinerating her.

Torryn ran up to her, gave her a hug, picked her up and said, "It's time to go."

Ingrid nodded, then Torryn threw her over the cliff. As soon as she fell into the ocean, the waves begun to drag her down below, making sure she couldn't escape. As she swam under the waves, a sensation came over her...a sensation she never felt before.

Chapter 19

A COUPLE OF MONTHS had gone by since the funeral was held, and Arthur having been turned into ashes and buried. Ingrid sat in Mathew's truck, listening to the heater blasting in the cabin as they stayed warm. The scenery that surrounded them was beautiful, and for Ingrid this was unknown territory. The both thought it would be best to go on a little trip to Norway, taking his truck along for the ride, so they could both work out their issues.

"Sure is beautiful," Ingrid said as she looked out the window.

"Yes, it is." Mathew agreed as he looked over at her. "I have a surprise for you."

"What is it?"

"You'll see."

Continuing over the bridge, Mathew could see the destination he had wanted to show Ingrid: Hamnoy, one of the islands he had heard about from one of his friends who had been there before. Once off the bridge, he parked the truck over by the piers and turned it off.

"What's going on?" Ingrid asked, looking puzzled.

"Get out, I'll show you." He smiled.

As they both got out, they started walking near the edge and just enjoyed the scenery. Ingrid took a deep breath, letting the cool wind into her system.

"Where are we?"

"Hamnoy. It's a little island here in Norway."

"It is unique, feels like I've been here before."

"Really?"

"Yes, I don't know why, but it feels like it. I've never been to Norway though."

"That's interesting."

They continued to walk around, closer to the ocean in complete silence, hand in hand.

Stopping for a moment, Ingrid turned towards the mountains that were surrounded by the ocean. A smile illuminated her face, then faded. Delicate snowflakes floated down, and a scene she had once seen before rose up before her eyes. Her chest tightened, and the sensation of her stomach dropping rang throughout her entire body. Mathew looked at her, confused and worried about what was going on.

"Are you okay?" he asked with concern in his voice.

After a moment, she finally replied, "Yes, I'm fine. I've just seen this before."

Silence saturated the air, creating an unusual sensation between them.

After a while, Mathew said that he was going to go check into the cabin they were renting, leaving Ingrid by herself on the shore to enjoy the scenery a little bit longer. As she stood there, a wave of emotions washed over her. It had been so long—over a decade—since she had experienced these emotions. Happiness, contentment, and safety flooded her, making her smile at the thought of where she was in her life. She had begun to accept that her dad was gone. She knew he was now safe and healed, and that made her happy for him. Inside her mind she felt safe—more than she ever had felt in her life.

Closing her eyes, Ingrid took a deep breath, letting her body become vulnerable to the elements around her. As she opened her eyes once more to look at the scene before her, the mournful song of the ocean lured her. As she walked towards the water, she did not fight her own body or mind. Slowly, she walked into the water fully clothed, not giving a damn about anything. The water hit her ankles, then her hips, and finally it was up to her shoulders. The water cradling her body gently, letting her know that she would be alright. Without looking back at the shoreline, she ducked below the water, letting herself become fully submerged.

Mathew had been walking back to the shore as Ingrid had been walking into the water, and his fears compelled him to run. Yelling frantically, trying to get her back to the shore did not help, because by the time he got to the edge of the water, Ingrid was already below the water. Panicking, Mathew started running full-speed into the merciless water.

"Ingrid! Where are you?"

Silence. Only the cruelty of silence. Then a voice.

"Mathew?"

He scoured the area to find Ingrid swimming in the water towards him…As she got closer to the shore, she could stop swimming and start walking towards him. Standing in front of Mathew, Ingrid placed her wet hands on his face.

"I'm okay, I promise," she said, her voice rippling with Zen, before kissing him gently.

Mathew wrapped his arms around her, not caring if he got soaked in the process. Placing a kiss on the top of her head, his eyes focused on the scenery of the mountains ahead, while Ingrid's eyes had seen a familiar face in the water: The sweet penguin... symbol of salvation. After a while, the penguin disappeared, and Ingrid smiled as she hugged Mathew a little tighter.

About the Author

LONI HOOTS is the author of four books of poetry: *The Nymph of the Unknown Forest, Beyond the Pillars, Songs of the Mist,* and *Hearts of Glass.*

She has also authored a children's book: *Little Bird, Little Bird,* (illus. Melissa Rohr) - the first of a series in the making.